SONG BREAKER

Other Works by
Annette Lyon

Novels
Lost Without You
At the Water's Edge
House on the Hill
At the Journey's End
Spires of Stone
Tower of Strength
Band of Sisters
Band of Sisters: Coming Home
A Portrait for Toni
The Golden Cup of Kardak

In the Newport Ladies Book Club Series:
Paige
Ilana's Wish
Tying the Knot

Novellas
Timeless Romance Anthology Series
Timeless Regency Collection: A Midwinter Ball
Timeless Victorian Collection: Summer Holiday
The Royals of Monterra: Tailor Made
Hazel of Heber Valley

Nonfiction
There, Their, They're: A No-Tears Guide to Grammar from the Word Nerd (1st and 2nd editions)
Done & Done: The Power of Accountability Partnering for Reaching Your Goals, cowritten with Luisa Perkins
Chocolate Never Faileth

SONG BREAKER

Bring your own song!

Annette Lyon

BLUE GINGER BOOKS

For Luisa

Malicious magic has been done;
Cause enough there is for crying,
To lament the magic malice.
This is why I'll weep forever,
What I'll mourn throughout my lifetime:
That I gave my sister Aino,
Even pledged my mother's child
To Väinämöinen as a helpmate
And provider for the singer.

Kalevala Runo 3: The Contention
Translated by Eino Friberg

Finnish Pronunciation Guide

While Finnish grammar is complex, the spelling and pronunciation is straightforward and phonetic. If you know what sound a letter makes, you can pronounce any word.

A few tips:
- J makes an English Y sound.
- The first syllable of a word is always stressed, with every other syllable thereafter getting a stress. Every letter is pronounced. Double vowels are held out longer, as with PAAVO.
- Double consonants are also held out longer, as with the name of Aino's sister, SANNA, and the wizard SEPPO.
- The letter Ä makes the same sound as an English short A, as in APPLE.

Diphthongs
Finnish has many diphthongs (and two vowels that don't exist in English, plus diphthongs that use those vowels!).

Below are a few simple diphthongs that appear frequently in the book that are easy for English speakers because the resulting pronunciation is simply a long vowel.

OU
The Finnish O sounds like a long English O, as in NOTE. The letter U makes an English OO sound, as in BOOT. Put them together, and the resulting pronunciation is much like the exclamation of "OH!" held out, which English speakers tend to

think of as a regular long O. It's really does include an OO at the end. This diphthong (long O + OO) appears in the name JOUKO.

AI

Finnish A's have an AH sound (as in BOX). Finnish I's make a long E sound, as in BEET. When put together (AH + EE), the resulting diphthong is what English speakers call a long I, heard in the word MICE. Hence, our heroine's name, AINO, is pronounced EYE-no.

AU

As with the AI diphthong, here we have an A (AH, as in BOX), followed by a U (OO in BOOT). The resulting diphthong (AH+OO) is pronounced OW as in COW. Turns out that the most commonly known Finnish word in the world, SAUNA, is chronically mispronounced. The first syllable rhymes with COW.

Character Name
Pronunciation Guide

Key to Pronunciation Guide:
OO = as in BOOT
O = long vowel as in BOAT
A = short vowel as in APPLE

An H after a vowel indicates a short vowel in English, such as AH or EH.

Major Characters Named in the *Kalevala*
Aino [EYE-no]
Vane (Full name: Väinämöinen)
Jouko [YOH-OO-ko] (Full Name: Joukahainen)
Seppo Ilmarinen (often just Ilmarinen) [SEHP-po IHL-mah-Reenen]
Sun and Moon Maids/Sisters

Major Characters Not Named in the *Kalevala*
Eva [EH-vah]—Seppo's wife
Kari [KAH-ree]—tietäjä/soothsayer/priest/hare
Paavo [PAAH-vo] Aino's love interest
Sanna [SAHN-nah]—Aino's older sister

Minor Characters Named in the *Kalevala*
Antero Vipunen [AHN-ter-o VEE-poo-NEN]
Louhi [LOH-OO-hee]
Maid of the North [Finnish: *Pohjolan Neito*]

Minor Characters/Names Not in the *Kalevala*
Antti [AHNT-tee]—Blacksmith, Katrina's husband
Ari [AH-ree]—Village elk hunter
Hannu [HAHN-noo]—Wizard who wrote of reversing spells
Katrina [KAH-tree-nah]—Antti's wife
Leo & Tuuli Pekkanen [LEH-o & TOO-lee PEHK-kah-nen]
    —Husband and wife villagers
Luoma, Mrs. [LOO-O-mah] — Berry merchant
Marjala [MAHR-yah-lah] — The fictional village. Literally, a
    place with berries
Matti [MAHT-tee]—Woodcutter
Milla [MEEL-lah]—Laundress
Mika [MEE-kah]—Villager with a broken plow
Pertti [PEHRT-tee]—Villager Jouko fells pines for

Finnish Terms

Juhannus [YOO-hah-noos]
Midsummer Night, during the summer solstice, the longest day of the year, when even at night, it's not dark.

Mämmi [MAM-mee]
A traditional Finnish dessert made of malted rye. Today, it's made for Easter and served with sugar and cream. In the story, it's made for the spring equinox celebration and served with honey and cream.

Piimä [PEE-ma]
A type of buttermilk/drinkable yogurt popular in Finland and other Nordic countries.

Pulla [POOL-lah]
A sweet bread flavored with cardamom

Sauna [SAH-OO-nah]
(The first syllable rhymes with COW. See *diphthongs*, above.)
The traditional Finnish steam bathhouse, an important part of the culture, hygiene, and even early survival. Finns have no sensual/sexual connotations with the sauna. Rather, the sauna is considered to be a place to put worldly things aside. As such, Finns find "bath houses" in other countries that include such things to be offensive.

Solki [SOL-kee]
A brooch worn by a betrothed young woman

Tietäjä [TEE-EH-ta-ya]
In pagan times, a soothsayer, seer, and priest. One who gained visionary abilities from the underworld, often from near-death experiences and/or from ancestors who have already passed. Translated literally, one who knows/a knower.

Vihta [VEEH-tah-yah]
A bundle of thin birch branches tied at the base. They are dipped in a bucket of water in the sauna and used to gently beat the skin, which is refreshing and invigorating. Eino Friberg calls them "slappers" in his English translation.

Writ Rock—The English term Eino Friberg used for a rock with sacred carvings on it.

Chapter One

"Daughter, look. Over there. Now!" Not content with ordering Aino about, Mama added a few sharp elbow jabs into her ribs. "Look, child!"

Aino had not celebrated nineteen birthdays without learning that her mother tended to grow overly excited about small matters. But when Mama's voice reached an unusually high pitch, Aino surrendered to the request.

"What is it?" She rubbed the sore spot on her side as she turned to look.

Surrounded by deep green pines, the village marketplace buzzed with an undercurrent of thrilled urgency. Townspeople of all ages poked and prodded one another, whispering with hushed excitement and pointing across the way. Even old Milla, the laundress, as sentimental as a block of ice, smiled and flushed—flushed! What could have made the town behave so foolishly?

"What is it, Mama?" Aino clutched a pelt she'd been considering for purchase. She stood on her toes, trying to peer above and around the thickening crowd.

The elbow jabs changed to incessant pats on Aino's arm—less painful, but no less of an annoyance. "It's not *what* is over there," her mother said impatiently. "But *who*."

"Who," Aino repeated, confused.

She'd assumed that someone had spotted a wolf, perhaps. Or that a group of unruly young men had started a brawl after one too many beers, even if it was a mite early in the day for alcohol.

An unexpected visitor or group of visitors, then. That was the only explanation. The village of Marjala had no residents of its own who could elicit such a level of excitement. Who could it be?

"Let's go look," Aino said, placing a hand over her mother's in the hopes that the gesture would put an end to the constant pats. "Shall we?"

"Yes, and hurry," Mama said. She behaved the part of a four-year-old promised a sweet bun for good behavior.

Aino turned to replace the pelt on a stack of furs at Mr. Sorsa's table. "Thank you. I'll probab—"

But even the fur merchant didn't seem to hear her; his attention had been drawn by the same commotion. Aino craned her head one way and then the other, past rows of vendor booths and tables, without success.

Had her mother actually seen the visitor? Or had she only heard about the man. Or was it a woman?

Mama leaned in. "It's Vane," she said in an awed whisper. She gripped both of Aino's shoulders. "Did you hear me? *Vane!*"

Though her shoulders smarted from the pressure of Mama's thumbs, Aino's eyes widened. "How can that be?" She noted that her own voice had grown breathless from surprise and awe.

How could the most powerful wizard in the world, both past and present, a man of legends and bedtime tales, be here in such a tiny, unimportant town as Marjala? Such a visitor would certainly be cause for a flurry of attention—if this visitor was truly Vane.

The throng grew by the moment, as if news of the wizard's appearance had traveled through the air to far-flung homes on the borders of the village, beckoning villagers to come. Grown women, young and old, fanned themselves as Mama did, ready to collapse in a faint at the prospect of seeing the old man. Even the boys and men seemed dazed, transfixed.

Everyone but Aino, it seemed. She'd never given the wizard much thought beyond the old tales she'd grown up with. What else could Vane be to her, when the stories told of such outlandish, impossible feats? He was said to sing the most powerful magic ever known. The tales claimed that he was nearly as old as the world itself, and had been born an old man hundreds of years in age but stronger than anyone, young or old.

Aino took her mother's hand and slowly picked their way through the crowd toward whatever spectacle awaited them.

It can't be Vane. If he were a real man from the past, surely the tales were exaggerated, and he'd long-since died. But if he were alive, he'd never come to somewhere as inconsequential as Marjala. The very idea was fancy and foolishness.

She gently pushed past Leo Pekkanen and his wife, Tuuli. "Excuse me," Aino said, but neither seemed to notice them.

"Are we almost there?" Mama pled like child.

"I don't know." Aino dearly hoped to get this nonsense over with, to learn of the interloper who'd so disturbed the market. The man needed to be sent on his way, whoever he was. Perhaps he was really a different grand wizard they'd never heard of. Had the man claimed to be Vane, or did someone make assumptions?

Then, despite her attempts at logic and reason, her mind posed a question. *What if the man truly is the Vane of legend?*

The thought should have seemed ridiculous, but the more Aino pressed through the crowd—surely Marjala didn't have so many people—the more the question burned into her mind.

No one had ever seen Vane, not in her lifetime, or her parents'. Of course, rumors of sightings circulated through the thick woods. Traders and travelers along rivers exchanged such tales, no doubt exaggerating the yarn each time it was retold.

But those tales were usually four or five steps removed from the person who'd supposedly caught a glimpse of the bushy-bearded wizard singing an unknown charm as he drove his famed sleigh. She'd heard not a word to convince her that he lived—now or ever. That he breathed and sang magic.

Ever since Aino had grown old enough to wear long skirts and tie her braids up in ribbons as grown women did, she'd assumed that the reason no one ever saw Vane was the simple fact that he'd died generations ago. His name and the grand deeds he'd supposedly done could easily have been invented by village storytellers and passed along, generation to generation.

How could he be real, when he was said to have been singing magic since before her great-grandparents were born? They'd long since been laid beneath the cold, dark earth. Yet she was supposed to believe that Vane lived today?

Aino wound through the crowd as quickly as she could. Aside from the need to calm her mother's excitement—worse than a puppy intent on jumping all over you—Aino felt an odd pull to move along, to confirm with her own faculties that the visit was not Vane of old, merely a wayward traveler with a long beard who looked like the man pictures in old drawing. Mama clung to Aino and squeezed her hand painfully; the knuckles rubbed together.

At last, the visitor came into view—a leathery-faced, wrinkled man with a long, gray beard as big as a shrub and likely as scratchy. He looked very old, yet his shoulders likely measured as wide as Aino and her mother side by side. His muscular arms had to be thicker than some tree branches.

Mama squealed and swatted Aino's arm. "It's Vane. It *is* him. I never imagined I'd see the day. Is my kerchief on straight?"

"It's fine," Aino said, hardly sparing a glance at her mother's head scarf. Mama, a married woman with grown children, behaved like a girl admiring a virile, young man of twenty. She'd gained a plump middle and deep wrinkles from constant scowls, but now she gazed with adoration upon an aged man who needed a bath and handfuls of leaves picked out of his beard.

Mama had always been calm and direct, often blunt to a fault, and never giddy or silly like "some porridge-brained young thing," as she called girls who concerned themselves with little more than whether they were noticed by handsome boys.

With disbelief, Aino looked back at the villagers. Men and women alike seemed charmed in their admiration, as if this man were a demigod and had put them under a spell.

Then again, if this is Vane, he might have.

The old man sampled berries from Mrs. Luoma—cloudberries, blueberries, blackberries, tiny wild strawberries.

4

He nodded here and there as juice ran from his chin into his beard. Mrs. Luoma rarely allowed anyone to sample her wares. Yet today she stood as still as a tree on a windless day. The man could have eaten his fill without a word from her.

He did have a powerful bearing, Aino had to concede. Legends sung around fires at night said that Vane had been born of Ilmatar, Queen of the Air. With such a parentage, he might well possess every scrap of power the stories claimed.

Assuming Vane exists at all. Yet she found a kernel of belief begin to swell inside her. Was she coming under the man's spell too? Deliberately, she looked away and blinked several times, as if that would cut off any influence the man might have had on her.

How did he create such a transfixed audience when he wasn't singing? Aino drew a step closer and then another. Now she stood close enough to hear, even with the murmur of the villagers, a deep hum from the man's barrel chest. He *was* singing a deep, resonating magic that seemed to surround him like a cloud.

He *was* a wizard, then. But was he the one who possessed songs so powerful they could fold the earth upon itself?

"Get closer," Mama said, a hand at her heart as if to calm its erratic beat.

Aino shook her head and held an arm out to hold her mother back. They already stood only a few strides away. Any closer, and the wizard might sing a curse their direction.

The air buzzed with an energy she couldn't define. The visitor had undoubtedly earned the title of wizard. Aino could feel the depth of his magic.

Marjala couldn't bear to have a curse sung onto their heads for not receiving a traveler properly. With a greater sense of unease, Aino prayed to the skies—to Ilmatar—that no one would upset the man, whatever his true name, even if he was born of the queen of the air. The gods rarely held to loyalty, even to their kin.

He's likely passing through, Aino assured herself. *This will all be over soon.*

Aloud she whispered to her mother, with the hope that no one—least of all the wizard, who tossed plump blueberries

5

into his mouth one by one—would hear. "Marjala already has a wizard, one who sleeps under our very roof every night."

"Your brother is very good—the best in the village," Mama agreed. She turned to look upon the wizard again. "But Jouko is nothing beside *Vane*." She spoke the last with a sigh.

Aino tried again. "You've said yourself that Jouko is the best singer you've ever heard." A tremor had entered Aino's voice, which belied her optimistic words.

She heartily wished she'd stayed behind at Mr. Sorsa's tables. Choosing a pelt sounded like a much better use of her time and attention, especially if it meant a chance to see his son, Paavo.

The visitor won't curse the village, she assured herself. *And no one will displace my brother.*

From behind his father, Paavo spotted her and quickly abandoned whatever chore he'd been assigned. With a broad smile on her face, he crossed to her and looked about for an excuse to speak to her. He grabbed a nearby fur. "Good to see you this morning, Aino. If you are in search of for something special, look at this. It's one of our newest. I guessed you might like it."

She reached for it, and their hands touched. Aino felt her cheeks blush. "Oh, I do like it," she said, looking at him, not the fur. "I like it very much."

Neither of them wanted to pull away. With Mama's attention on Vane, they didn't need to. They couldn't risk a long conversation, however, so this short moment would have to suffice for the day. Paavo shot her one of his wide grins, then winked and headed back to his father's table.

Chapter Two

Aino watched Paavo retreat until the crowd had swallowed him. Mama had begun moving side to side to prevent others from blocking her view of the wizard. He stood below an awning of pine branches. She held an arm out to the side to guard her position.

"Mama," Aino tried again. "You've said countless times that Jouko is the best singer you've ever heard, remember? We don't need another."

Her mother didn't look at her, just gazed at the old man. "Your brother's skills are fine, I suppose."

Fine, she supposes?

It was a rare day when Mama didn't brag about the wizard she'd brought into the world. "But then I've never heard Vane singing. Think what grand feats he could do with his voice! Charms we can only dream of."

His leather boots kicked up pine needles across the mossy forest floor as the wizard moved on from the berry booth. The crowd parted to let him through. He paused beside a booth with baskets of vegetables piled high. With a leathery hand, Vane took a handful of new potatoes and bit into one as if it were an apple. No one said a word about payment.

As he chewed, he turned toward the crowd, amusement toying with the corners of his mouth. Suddenly Aino could see the pattern on his leather pouch. Men and women alike wore such pouches from their belts, often with embroidered patterns that hailed from their native areas. The colors and designs held meaning. Every pouch became a statement of identity and heritage.

She'd never seen a pouch like this one. Instead of rows of patterned stitching, it bore a single image: a square with a round twist in each corner. As he moved around the crowd to another booth, Aino stared at the design embroidered in red on a blue background.

It can't be.

But there was no mistaking it: he indeed wore the Braid of Fate.

The pouch bore witness to the only explanation: this was Vane. No one else would dare wear that symbol. In all of history, only one person had ever worn it. The Braid of Fate showed that Vane had power over everything, even his future.

Many stories claimed that Vane's flagrant display of the Braid of Fate was the greatest impudence, that it tempted the gods. Others grudgingly admitted that, while wearing the Braid was a sign of conceit, it was also little more than a statement of fact. Vane *was* the most powerful wizard the world had ever seen. He *did* have power over his future. The Braid served to warn to others as much as anything.

He'd skirted the edge of the crowd, past Aino and her mother. People approached him in a way Aino hadn't desired to—or dared. Mama looped her arm through Aino's and drew the two of them toward Vane again. She pushed and shoved to gain better vantage. Uneasy, Aino glanced back at Paavo. If only she could stay behind and talk with him while her mother and the rest of the villagers made fools of themselves.

When they were close to the front again, Mama huffed with satisfaction. "Much better." She released Aino's arm then smoothed her skirts.

Near him, an elderly woman with a red- and white-checkered scarf about her head called out a request. "Please, sir, sing just a small phrase." She reached out as if to touch his sleeve but pulled back before contact. "Just a few notes?" Awe dripped from every word. "Make some pinecones dance, perhaps? I wouldn't want to wear you out."

A young man from halfway back had no such concerns. "Make my sister howl like a wolf!" He pointed toward a girl of about twelve. His sister's eyes went wide. She reached for her throat and stared at Vane. The singer chuckled at the suggestion and dismissed the request as he had the first.

A middle-aged man called out with a strong voice. "Sir, I'll pay you to make broken plow straight. It struck a rock and bent Friday last."

"No, sing about your mother, Ilmatar, about her part in the creation of the world," someone else suggested.

Once again Vane laughed—a booming sound. He shook his head; his wiry beard swayed. "I'm not here to sing." His voice sounded like gravel. "If you'll all excuse me." He stepped forward, and the crowd parted again as he made his way to another booth.

A cool breeze kicked up, and though his long hair flew about wildly, his black cap didn't budge. He paused again and eyed hanks of hand-dyed yarn. The owners of the booth, an elderly couple, exchanged incredulous—yet thrilled—looks.

Clutching his wife's hand, the husband took off his hat and said, "May I—help you?"

"When was the last time Vane ventured out of the southern woods?" Mama whispered loudly, swatting Aino's arm again. "I doubt anyone in *any* village has seen him all winter long, and now he graces *our* market!"

Aino didn't answer; her mother didn't expect one. Instead, she simply crossed her arms, purposely covering the sore spot. But she pondered her mother's question.

What *did* Vane mean by his visit to Marjala? Beyond creating plenty of gossip, what did his presence matter, especially if he wouldn't perform a single charm?

She looked up, past the trees around them, to the blue sky, and again pled, *Ilmatar, don't let your son curse us.*

Could she convince her mother to move to the Sorsas' booth? Aino could likely slip away, but she didn't dare leave her mother alone, not when she was liable to say something that might stir up Vane's anger enough to curse the town.

She yearned for more time with Paavo. His nearness always made her feel safe, and there in the market, staring at Vane, she would have given much to calm the heavy uneasiness pressing against her chest.

She surreptitiously looked at the table of furs and caught Paavo's eye. He smiled, and she wanted to run into his arms even more. Instead, Aino forced herself to remain by her mother's side. She smiled back and bit her lip with pleasure.

Ever since they could walk, she and Paavo had known each other. They'd skated on the same ponds in winter. They'd swum in the same lakes in the summer. But now that they were grown, they'd come to see each other oh so differently.

For her part, she'd found that his broadened shoulders and smooth, deepened voice drew her near and made her heart pound. His smiles made her cheeks warm and a flurry of butterflies erupt in her middle.

She eyed Vane and then Paavo again. The wizard seemed no closer to singing a charm or a curse than before. Perhaps she could slip her mother away without a scene.

Aino leaned close to her mother's ear and whispered, "I want to see that silver fox pelt again. It would make such a pretty muff for you next winter." To convince her further, Aino added, "I noticed a nice piece of leather that would be perfect for a new pair of shoes for you." The urge to leave had grown into a desperation. The heaviness grew until it felt like a granite boulder on her best, withholding air.

Mama tore her gaze from Vane and gripped Aino's arm—so hard she nearly gasped—and leaned in. "We will stay right here. Vane must have a reason for coming today. This is important."

"But he's not here to sing; he said so himself."

The words seemed to penetrate her mother's mind enough for her to at least consider them. Aino held her breath and glanced back at Paavo, clinging to hope.

Mama's attention settled on the wizard, and her eyes had a glassy look. Aino didn't speak again, didn't plead; she simply put her arm around mother's shoulders and guided her a step away. Aino took another step, and another, and another. Her mother gradually moved with her, she still admiring the wizard.

"Vane looks even stronger than the stories," her mother said. She pressed a hand to her heart. "I'm sure he's even more wealthy, too. Isn't he handsome?" She sighed dramatically.

Aino's eyebrow went up. Strong as an ox Vane might be; his forearms had cords of muscles and were larger around than her legs. But *handsome?* No. There was a reason Vane known in all the stories as *Old Reliable*. Although the title was one of respect, it hadn't been given entirely for that reason.

Vane was old—so very old. Aged centuries, if the tales were true. Even with magic, Aino couldn't imagine how that was possible.

Perhaps if she were older, she might see him as the older townswomen did. Her mother certainly didn't seem to be the only middle-aged woman fawning over the old man. They believed him capable of magic one could only dream of. Perhaps he carried an air of magic around him wherever he went, and that's why the women behaved so foolishly.

Aino recalled some of the tales about Vane: How he could change the weather over an entire valley. Send rain for days during a drought. How crops he sang over grew faster and taller. Vane supposedly could heal even deadly diseases and injuries, as he had in the story about the girl who was attacked by a bear and nearly bled to death.

Few people ever saw Vane—and even fewer heard him sing, so no one knew how accurate the stories were. Surely most were exaggeration, but what parts held kernels of truth?

At last Aino reached the Sorsas' booth, and she could breathe normally again, though her mother's attentions were still directed at Vane, now a couple of stone throws away. Her mother played the fool—more so than the other villagers. Mama tended to be, well, outspoken, and that alone made any defense of the family's reputation a challenge. Her behavior today would make things ten times worse—she seemed downright drunk.

"Look at these skins. Aren't they nice?" Aino's attempt at distraction didn't work. Instead, she found her attention drawn to Vane again. And she gasped.

The old wizard looked right at *her*—smiled with arrogant amusement.

She sucked in a breath. He took a step in her direction, and the crowd parted. Every time his boots drew him closer, the granite in her chest grew heavier and larger. He drew closer; Aino had a hard time breathing at all and felt certain she'd faint dead away any moment.

Jouko, where are you? She wanted his help. Needed it.

Yet if he had been there, could he have saved her? Her brother could fix a broken plow, but even on his best days, he couldn't sing rain down onto more than a few paces' worth of a plowed field at a time. He certainly couldn't heal more than cuts or a clean break in a bone.

11

Vane was almost upon her, so close she could smell him—bear tallow, campfire smoke, with a moist, ferny odor mixed in. She tried to back away, but only backed into the table of furs. Tears of panic pricked her eyes. She frantically looked about her but couldn't find a way out—couldn't find even Paavo.

The crowd had hushed; all eyes were trained on Vane and his approach toward Aino. The only sounds were his steps on the forest floor and the crunch of pine needles beneath his leather boots.

Why was he giving *her* attention, when dozens of eager women would have gladly received it instead?

Aino reached back and gripped the edge of the table with both hands. She focused on the lichen-covered stones she stood on. If she'd known the wizard would be at the market, she'd have stayed home.

Two strides from her, Vane stopped, but his eyes never left her. One more step, and he could have reached out and touched her. The very idea made gooseflesh break out on her arms.

Please don't, she thought. *Please.*

Slowly, Vane looked to his right. He'd stopped beside the blacksmith's display. Vane's fingers trailed over polished handles and shiny metal blades. After a moment of consideration, he selected an ax. He turned it over in his hands, testing the weight and balance, studying the workmanship—the sturdy handle with engraved designs, the sharp blade. The merchant, Antti, swallowed hard and threw an uneasy glance to his wife, Katrina.

Vane lifted the ax as if to swing. The crowd backed away to give him room, eyes wide. The axe swooped through the air with precision. When he tossed it above his head, an audible gasp went through the crowd. The axe spun around overhead, making three full circles before Vane suddenly reached out and grasped it out of the air.

"I'll take it." He reached into his pouch and pulled out some coins. "I hope this is enough." He deposited several on the table.

Katrina scooped them into her hand and dropped them into her pouch. Had Vane cheated them, or been generous? In the end, the amount was of no concern; that would be all the blacksmith and his wife would get.

Perhaps the wizard hadn't meant to approach Aino after all; he'd just wanted an axe. She let out a huge sigh of relief and gripped a nearby birch branch to steady her knees.

But then, still at the blacksmith's table, Vane turned his head and gave Aino one more deep stare. She felt as if he could read her mind—and wanted her to know he'd noticed her.

From somewhere in the throng, a woman said hopefully, "Change the color of my cloak? It's such a dingy brown. I'd so like a pretty yellow."

Vane threw his head back and laughed as if she'd asked him to turn the sky purple. "I came only for a new ax." His voice was deep and raspy. "Rumor said your market has many quality goods. It is time I leave."

A chorus of disappointment rang out. Mama groaned audibly with the rest. Now that she knew the purpose of his visit, Aino narrowed her eyes, the heaviness now replaced with an odd curiosity.

Why wouldn't Vane sing even a few notes? How easy it would be for someone with his power to change the color of a cloak; that would require hardly any effort. What if his reluctance meant that he really *couldn't* do the kind of feats the stories bragged about? Perhaps his powers were no longer as strong—if they'd ever been.

His speaking voice was so rough that surely his singing had to sound the same.

Does a rough voice affect magic? I'll have to ask Jouko.

Vane adjusted his belt and hefted his ax over one shoulder. With a hand on the knife at his belt, one with a handle of reindeer-antler, he walked away from Aino. The crowd reverently parted, all watching his long, sure strides that were not ones of a man his purported age.

"Strong as an ox," Mama said beside Aino in a soft, wistful voice. "Oh, what I wouldn't do for such a man." She glanced over askance, as if realizing that she'd embarrassed herself. She coughed and added, "A man for—a—a *son-in-law*, naturally. What a catch he would be for *you* or *your sister*." She turned around, clapped her hands and turned to the Sorsas' table once again.

Aino didn't join her. This time, it was her gaze fixed on Vane. She wouldn't feel at ease until he'd left the marketplace altogether and she couldn't see his figure any longer. When he reached the edge of the market, he didn't step into the dense forest beyond. Instead, he paused for the space of a breath, then slowly turned about.

His stroked his beard one, twice, then walked back to the market—straight toward Aino. Mama glanced over her shoulder, noted the wizard, and whirled around. A sound between a squeal and a squawk escaped her. "He's—he's—" was all she could say before she whipped around to study fur pelts again.

The lump of granite on Aino's chest returned, this time heavier than ever. She could scarcely stand. Her knees trembled with every step he took.

He stopped an arm's reach away. "You, my dear," he said to Aino with his gravelly voice, "are a pretty girl."

She clutched a raccoon pelt so hard she feared she might tear it. "Thank you, um, sir." What else could she say or do?

At the sound of his voice, her mother abandoned all pretense of inspecting furs. She faced him and curtseyed deeply. "Old Reliable Vane, it is an honor to see you and to speak to you." Her manner seemed far more controlled than Aino would have expected, but the wizard didn't seem to notice her at all.

Instead, he touched Aino's arm. A spark traveled up to her shoulder, to her scalp, down to her toes, and back to her chest, where her heart seemed to literally skip a beat. Aino had to restrain a cry at the sudden pain.

Vane spoke again, this time louder, to Paavo's father. "I'll want your best fox pelt. It is for this girl"—he nodded at Aino—"for her to make herself a fine hat to wear this winter."

Mr. Sorsa's face went pale. He seemed paralyzed, unable to respond. Paavo somehow managed to search through the stacks and withdraw the largest and most magnificent silver fox pelt Aino had ever seen. She stood there stunned, unable to grasp what was happening. Her only thought was that her winter hats had always been of rough reindeer or soft rabbit fur, never of rare and expensive silver fox.

The old man eyed the fur. "That will do," he said, as if the flawless piece were somehow inferior. He dropped a gold coin into Paavo's hand. Then a second and a third and fourth.

Now it was Paavo's eyes that widened as big as rounds of rye bread. It was Paavo's body that became paralyzed. Those coins could feed the Sorsa family all winter—longer, even.

Vane gently pressed the pelt into Aino's reluctant hands. "A pretty gift for a pretty girl." The painful jolt of magic didn't rush through her again, but perhaps that was because the pelt separated them. Before, he'd touched her skin.

She could do nothing but hold the pelt to her chest and stare as Vane walked away and—this time—disappeared into the thick pines.

The spell of his presence wore off almost as quickly as it came. Mr. Sorsa shook his head as if clearing cobwebs from it. He turned to Mama. "Did you want a reindeer skin?"

"Uh, yes. I do." She looked confused, as if she'd woken from a dream. "I think." But she was distracted by the fox pelt in Aino's hands. Her mother stroked it as if it were a pet. Aino wanted to shove it into her mother's arms and never touch—or see it—again.

"Paavo," Mr. Sorsa said over his shoulder to his son, "go find the other reindeer skins like this one."

"Yes, Papa." Paavo threw a wink Aino's way, then ducked under the table. This time his wink didn't set the butterflies aflutter. They couldn't fly about when the granite boulder weighed inside her.

Aino turned uneasily in the direction Vane had gone. She could make him out yet; the red band of his cap stood out through the trees.

As if he could feel her gaze, his step slowed, stopped. He turned around. Aino held her breath against the dread pounding through her veins. In spite of the distance, she could see every detail of his deeply lined face. He looked right at her, and his gaze pierced her to the core.

He can't make me out in the crowd, surely.

15

Yet his mouth slowly widened into a broad smile, and he nodded toward her in acknowledgment, then pointed at the pelt in her hands.

Her heart felt ready to hop out of her chest. Had he assumed she watched his departure,

or had he *known* it? Did it matter? Why did he take note of her, instead of dozens of others?

And why had he bought her a pelt for a hundred times what it was worth? After what felt like an eternity facing the table of furs, she dared peer over her shoulder.

Vane still stood in the distance, gaze locked on her. He nodded again, then raised a hand in a sharp wave. Aino found herself lifting a hand in a gesture of farewell. Only then did he turn and continue his journey along the forest path between the blueberry bushes, which drooped under the weight of their fruit.

Strength nearly spent, Aino shuddered and leaned against the table.

Distinguished and well-respected Vane might be—and rich—but he was also wrinkled and rough and . . . so *old*. He had brittle and yellow nails, rough palms, and no interest in anything a young woman like her would care about.

Mama would like him for a son-in-law, would she?

Marriage to such a man could curl a girl's toes and turn her hair gray before its time. She reached up and ran a hand along the loops of one of her braids, which were tied with green ribbons. What would it be like to be forced to marry Vane—or any man? She'd have to cover up her gorgeous red hair as a proper married woman must.

I will cover my head for no man but Paavo.

Yet even he wouldn't ask for her hand until he had his own land and could care for her. That could be years away. Paavo reappeared with two more reindeer skins, one larger than the other.

"Very good, son," Mr. Sorsa said, taking the skins from Paavo. "Now go fetch our midday food. I'm famished." He laid the skins out for her mother to admire.

Paavo dutifully nodded and headed into the woods to fetch the wraps, which likely in the shade of a nearby tree to keep them cool. Only after she could no longer see him did Aino hand Vane's silver pelt to her mother.

To calm her worries, Aino whispered to herself. "Sanna will marry first."

Mama moved the fox pelt to her other arm and leaned over to inspect the reindeer skins. "I suppose your sister will marry first. The elder daughter usually does, you silly girl." She lowered a skin, patted it, and said, "I'll take all three."

Her mother's earlier words weren't entirely comforting. Sanna lacked suitors of any kind. The longer it took for her to find a husband, the longer Aino and Paavo had to wait to be wed.

But for some reason, the order mattered, as if the assurance of the proper order would lift the weight of the boulder still on her chest.

Vane's pelt felt like a sign of doom. Aino found her hands trembling with anxiety and looked away from the pelt, as if a different view would help her think rationally. She had no reason to believe that anyone had the desire to take her to wife.

Vane himself had been married at least twice already and outlived both wives. But if he wanted another, why would he look in the direction of an eighteen-year-old girl?

She had no reason to think such a thing—except for the queer heaviness that filled her entire chest. Except for the fact that he'd noted her especially. He'd bought her a gift. And he'd paid more for it than her family made in a year.

What haunted her most was that Mama had said she would like Vane as a son-in-law.

Thoughts had little power. But words . . . *words* held deep power, a type of deep magic no one fully understood. The moment a thought left a person's lips, it received that power.

Therefore, one should *never* speak certain words unless you wanted them to happen—and even then, one often learned that a wish that became reality wasn't what you truly wanted.

"You wouldn't give permission for me to marry first?"

Her mother looked up from her coin purse with a jolt. "You, getting married?" She put a hand on one hip and turned to face Aino, brows raised, which made the wrinkles in her forehead turn into deep furrows.

"You're far too young for such nonsense." She lowered her voice so the merchant wouldn't hear. "Do you have a suitor? It had better not be Paavo." She jerked her head the young man's direction. Aino shot a look at him; he blushed and tried to pretend he hadn't heard. "Since last Midsummer Eve, he's been batting his eyes at you like a stray fawn." She wagged a finger at Aino. "I'll have none of it until you're older. Do you understand?"

"Yes, Mama." Aino hid a smile of relief and smiled at Paavo. "Thank you."

One of these days, she'd change her mother's opinion of him. For now, all that mattered was that Sanna would be the first to marry.

Chapter Three

A week had passed since Vane's appearance at the market, but based on the flurry of excitement that still wove through Marjala, that day at the market might as well have been but yesterday. The townspeople spoke of him constantly, whether to tell their own stories about what they'd seen—stories that grew more embellished by the day—or to speculate as to why he'd come at all.

The most popular idea was that the wizard might build a house nearby, in which case, they'd be able to come to him for help, and he'd sing his magic all the day long to fix their problems.

Aino had no such fantasies. She wished the singer had never come, or that someone would cast a spell over the town so they'd forget he'd ever appeared and life could return to the quiet existence Marjala was known for. Not that such a song existed. She stirred a big pot of pea soup for dinner, which, thanks to providence, had respectable chunks of chopped ham instead of the meager flecks that marked leaner years.

Behind her at the table, Mama chattered—about Vane, of course. For Aino, the topic had grown tiresome after a single day.

"I can't help but be jealous of Katrina and Antti." Mama laid wood bowls on the table for supper. "What an honor it would be to have Vane buy something from you . . . to know he's uses a tool *you* made?" She paused and hugged a bowl, dreamily staring at the wall. "If only your father had a ware to sell to such a man."

Aino had no idea how to respond, so she didn't. Fortunately, Mama didn't seem to expect an answer. She finished setting the table. After she clapped the last of the tin mugs into place, she wiped her hands on her apron, and then went to the counter to cut the bread. The rye slices would have to be thin; the family had to make their stores last until the harvest at the end of summer.

Aino's elder sister, Sanna, sat in a corner, knitting a pair of socks for their father. "I wonder how Vane learned his magic," she said. Her interest must have been piqued by Mama's never-ending chatter about him. "Maybe he could teach Jouko more enchantments to sing. Wouldn't *that* be an honor!"

"That would be a *dream*." Mama leaned against the table as if the idea made her knees weak.

Aino returned to the pot and stirred it vigorously. *If I can't escape talk of Vane from my mother, couldn't I at least escape it from my sister?* She'd hidden the silver pelt in a corner of the storage shed and had every intention of leaving it there.

"Is the soup ready?" Mama asked as she carried the bread basket to the table.

"We can eat as soon as Father and Jouko arrive." Aino tapped the wooden spoon on the edge of the pot.

From outside, they heard the shed door bang shut— likely Father putting away his tools; he'd be here shortly. A moment later, quick but heavy footsteps stormed up the porch, and the door opened, but Father didn't enter.

Rather, Jouko burst into the room. "I can't take it anymore!" He kicked the thick door shut behind him then yanked off his hat and shoved it onto a wall hook. With two long strides, he reached the table and dropped to the bench, nostrils flaring. Their brother was usually so easy-going. The sisters eyed each other uneasily.

Mama sat on the bench beside him. She looked calm, but her tone implied otherwise. For Jouko to be so upset, something must be terribly wrong. "What is it? Did something happen while you worked today?"

"You could say that," Jouko said with narrowed eyes. He pushed off the table; the mugs wobbled. Aino practically danced a couple of steps to the side and back to get out of his way as he paced the room. "*I* am the best singer in the village!" He jabbed his forefinger into his chest.

"Yes, dear, you certainly are." Mama hurried across the room and filled a mug with water from the pail, then brought it to him. "Here. Have some water. It will make you feel better."

When his only response was a scowl aimed at the fireplace, she added, "Did someone insult your singing?"

That was Aino's guess as well. She and her sister waited for him to reply, Jouko rarely let his temper out, but when he did, it might as well have been like a storm sent from the gods.

Jouko snatched the water and downed it in three gulps, and then he threw the tin mug against the wall.

Sanna hadn't left her spot on the chair, but her needles no longer moved. They remained still, and her knuckles had gone white. "Everyone knows you're the best singer in Marjala."

Again, he didn't speak. He hadn't lashed out at Sanna, so Aino ventured a step closer, head tilted in concern. "What is it, brother?"

"Vane." He smacked his fist against the wall, making Aino jump. "*He's* the matter." Jouko shot a fierce look Aino's direction.

"He's—he's back?" Aino asked, a hitch in her voice.

Mama's face flushed with repressed excitement. "Is he back?"

At Jouko's glare, their mother quickly replaced the look on her face with one of disinterest.

"He's not back, thank the skies," Jouko growled. He pushed off the wall and paced the cabin again. "But he might as well be. Everywhere I've gone over the last week, all I have heard is talk about Vane. This morning I stopped up the hole in the Laurinens' boat. It's perfectly watertight now, better than new."

"Did they not pay you?" Mama asked, bewildered.

"Oh, they paid me, but as I worked, Mrs. Laurinen watched the whole time and kept wondering how Vane would have fixed it if he'd been there instead. Faster, surely, or with a different, more effective technique, because he has more powerful words and tunes."

Aino sighed with relief. The fuss over Vane would end eventually, with no harm done. "That must be frustrating for you—"

"That doesn't cover it," Jouko snapped. "What does it matter *how* I fixed their boat if it's *fixed?*" He shoved both hands through his hair. "It's been the same complaint all week, no matter the job. How well I sang mattered not a lick. I felled eight pines for Pertti—that's two more than I'd ever done with a single song before. But that wasn't enough. To hear him speak of it, Vane could have felled all eight with four notes. This afternoon I fixed Mika's plow—and the entire time, he whined about how he'd asked Vane to fix it and had to *settle* for me."

Settle? No wonder Jouko was upset. Aino didn't blame him one bit.

He shook his head and pounded the wall with a fist. "They *all* talk about how much greater a singer Vane is, how much more powerful his songs are than mine. Yet none of them have ever heard him sing one note. I used to be respected here, but now . . ." Shoulders rounded, he trudged to the fireplace and leaned one arm against the mantel. He stared into the coals. "I'll be forever in his shadow."

The fire seemed to have burned somewhat out of his anger, so Aino crossed to him and put a hand on his arm. "They mean nothing by it. They're still excited over his appearance. Everyone in and around Marjala relies on you and your songs. We couldn't get by more than a day without your enchantments." She searched his face for some hint of softening, or comfort, but found none. "You are the best singer I've ever heard."

A sardonic smile played at the corners of his mouth. "Thank you, little sister, but I don't think this will pass, and I cannot abide it much longer. Some folks are quiet about it, but others say right to my face that I'm second best." He let out a heavy breath. "I didn't mind being second best as an apprentice. Seppo was a master. A comparison to him was an honor."

Mama sidled up to him, as if she'd gotten the courage to do so after Aino had come to him. "Since Seppo is old and can no longer sing . . . you really *are* the best singer within leagues."

"I'm the best *anywhere.*" Jouko's eyes flashed. "I know I'm the best. I must do something. I must prove to everyone that they have the best wizard right here in Marjala."

The heavy sensation Aino felt in the market returned to her chest. "No, brother." She could scarcely get enough air to say those words. She shook her head without any idea of what he was conjuring. It didn't matter; with his temper, whatever the scheme, it would be a mistake. "Don't do it. Whatever it is, you'll regret it the rest of your days."

Their mother waved away Jouko's concern. "No need to prove anything. The fervor will die down soon enough. As your sister said, the village needs your songs. In a few weeks, no one will speak of Old Reliable anymore. Now sit down, and I'll get you some soup." She turned about to fetch a ladle.

The door opened again, and Papa entered. He hung his jacket and cap on a hook then clapped his hands together. "Supper smells delicious."

"It's ready," Mama said. She held up the ladle. "Everyone, bring me your bowls."

Sanna and Aino obeyed, but Jouko stayed at the fireplace, brows knit together.

Their father went to him. "Son? What's wrong?"

After a moment, Jouko straightened and turned to Papa. The fury that had covered his face had melted into a cocky smile. "Nothing will be wrong for much longer. I know how to set it all right."

The heavy stone in Aino's chest sank to her middle and pulled her down to the bench. She sat there, hands over her stomach. *No, Jouko. No!*

She couldn't say that; he'd only dig his heels in deeper. "What are you planning to do?"

Mama filled his bowl with soup, and handed it to him. Jouko took it and dipped a finger into the soup. He licked it off and grinned. "I'm going to Vane's Knoll."

"You're *what?*" Papa asked. "You can't be in earnest—"

"And when I find him, we'll have a duel—man to man, song to song. We'll see who the better singer is. And when I come home victorious, no one will be able to dismiss my skills ever again. They will all know that *I* am the most powerful wizard in the world."

"I can't let you do this." Papa said it as if Jouko was still a boy and able to be controlled. Their parents exchanged worried looks, but they didn't look as panicked as Aino felt.

You don't tamper with magic! She wanted to yell the words. How foolish must her brother be to consider any kind of duel, let alone one with Vane? No one knew how strong he was, and if only half of the stories were true . . .

23

Suddenly cheerful, Jouko sat at the table and grabbed a spoon. "Why *shouldn't* I defend my name?"

Their father sat astride the bench and shoved the bowl out of Jouko's reach. "This isn't a matter of honor. You shouldn't go because—" His voice cut off as he seemed to search for a way to argue his point.

"Because why?" Jouko demanded.

"Because he's *Vane*." Papa softened his tone. "Vane is, well, older and far more experienced. He *is* more powerful. *No one* can sing like he can. Remember, he was *born* of magic. He bears powers no one else can possess, no matter how they study and practice." His gaze seemed to drill into Jouko's. For a moment, Aino held her breath and hoped her brother would see reason.

Instead, he replied tersely. "You used to say that *I* was the best." His eyes were hooded. Aino wished she could reach out and smooth away furrows in his brow and the bitterness that caused them.

"Oh, son," Papa said, shaking his head, "How can I make you understand? You *are* remarkably skilled, especially for a singer so young. I've never seen your equal of any age. Truly, never in my life." He scrubbed the back of a hand against his jaw. "Seppo was the best of teachers. Combine his instruction with the gifts of words and song that you were born with. You are truly remarkable."

Jouko's expression of distrust and frustration didn't change. He folded his arms and asked, "But?"

"But that doesn't mean you're better than Vane. I've never heard him sing. Neither has your mother, or anyone we know. If he's a tenth as powerful as the legends claim . . ." Papa shrugged. "Don't despair, my boy. I have no doubt that you will continue to grow in strength. In time, you may well be the better singer."

A momentary silence was cut short when Jouko lifted his chin in defiance. "Am I to thank you for that?"

"You're to be humble enough to see truth and to rein in foolish passions."

At that, Jouko snorted with disdain.

"Vane is more than a man." Papa placed a heavy hand on his son's shoulder; Jouko looked up. "If you contend with

Vane, he *will* win. I don't know how, but he'll make you suffer before declaring himself the victor."

Jouko seemed to be listening. Aino clasped her hands and prayed to Ilmatar that he'd see reason, perhaps take a swim in a cold lake or spend time in the sauna to clear his head.

"He's killed many men in many ways," Papa continued. "He could throw you into the water and drown you. He could tie you up and leave you to the mercy of the wild animals and the elements. He could sing snow upon you so you'd freeze to death."

At that Jouko grunted and turned back to his soup, but Papa forced him to look at him again, this time holding both shoulders. "Listen to me, son. If you challenge Vane, you will *die*. If you go, we'll pray that you never find him, because that will be the only way you will live."

Aino eyed her brother. He seemed to ponder Papa's words—or at least, he hadn't rejected them outright. She could almost see his mind turning like a miller's stone, round and round. Where would they stop?

"Don't do it," Aino said, so softly she wasn't sure anyone could hear her.

"Stay," Sanna pled, her knitting forgotten in her lap.

Mama picked up a slice of bread and slathered butter on it. She set it before Papa and took another. Her movements were fast, and the butter spread unevenly. "I have but one son." Her voice trembled, and she didn't look at Jouko or anyone else. She set a piece of buttered bread by Sanna's seat and began on another. "A son's duty is to protect the family name." The next piece of bread landed near Aino's bowl. Mama didn't take another. Instead she shoved the butter crock away and hit the table with her fist. "You will *not* make a mockery of this family."

Aino's eyes went wide. She looked from her mother to her brother and back again, bracing herself for a loud row. Her brother's face seemed to get redder by the second. Giving Jouko orders had never worked; didn't Mama know that?

Once more, Aino tried to appeal to his ego. "The villagers can't get along without you, not for one day."

"And Midsummer Eve is soon," Sanna added, latching on to Aino's argument. "You will be needed for all kinds of work—planting and repairs, and then the fall harvest, and of course, there are always illnesses and accidents—"

"And only a fool would seek out Vane for a duel," Mama finished.

Jouko strode about the room like a caged animal. "I was taught by *Seppo Ilmarinen.*"

"We know that, son," Papa said.

"The same Seppo who forged the sampo! Vane couldn't make the sampo. Only Seppo Ilmarinen could."

Or so say the legends.

"I was trained by the man who could forge what Vane could not." Her brother poked his own chest with a finger. "I was his apprentice."

"Yes, yes, of course," Papa said.

Could you forge a sampo? Aino knew the answer to that question—of course not. No one knew how Seppo Ilmarinen had managed to create the magical mill that churned gold, flour, and salt—everything needed for wealth and a good life.

But Jouko waved an arm, taking in the entire family. "You all think I'm second rate, don't you? None of you believes I can best Old Reliable." He kicked a chair and scowled.

"I believe in you." Aino said. Would that she could find the words to keep him home.

Jouko turned to look at her, eyebrows raised in obvious surprise. "You . . . do?"

"I've never doubted you. You are amazing. But even so, don't go. Sanna's right. How will the village get along without you for even a few days? Have pride in yourself. You have nothing to prove."

"Oh, but I do." He shook his head sadly. "I have everything to prove to myself." Jouko's tone had softened, but the determination was still there. "If I stay, I'll always wonder. So no, I will not cower from Vane like a scared little bird. I will seek out his knoll and challenge him."

He strode out the door and down the two porch steps, with Aino and the rest of the family close behind. He headed to the stable out back. Just as he grasped the handle of the door, Aino caught up and put her hand over his. He sighed wearily.

"Don't go," she begged. "Stay. For me."

The heaviness in her chest only grew; the weight pulled inside her so much she could scarcely stay upright. If Jouko left, something horrible would happen. She felt it deep in her bones.

"I *must* go." He almost sounded like the young boy Aino remembered from childhood—scared and vulnerable and stubborn as a rock. He peered into her face as if he could make her understand. The room was so quiet, so heavy, that the sound of a squirrel scratching its way across the roof seemed loud.

Aino broke the silence, knowing he'd made up his mind. Even so, she would keep trying, with the hope that her words wouldn't be powerless. "No. You don't have to go."

"But I *do*." Jouko turned about and looked from one family member to the next. He groaned in frustration. "Can't any of you see? I cannot live this way."

"Live *what* way?" Papa asked with exasperation.

"With the knowledge that others think less of me, that I'm weaker and less skilled than an old man." The pain in his face was genuine.

Mama snorted and folded her arms. "Vane is hardly some an old man."

When Jouko's jaw muscles tensed in response, Aino rushed in. "Contending with Vane is *not* the answer." She clung to his arm. Her heart pounded so hard it felt ready to tear into pieces. "Stay."

"He is *not* the stronger singer." Jouko's jaw worked as he stared through the trees at the gold and red of the sunset.

"Of course not," Aino said, not knowing—or caring—whether her statement was true. All that mattered was keeping Jouko from making a foolish mistake. She put a hand on her brother's cheek. He reluctantly turned his face toward hers. "We need you here, at home. The village needs you."

He looked over the family's freshly planted fields. Aino's gaze followed his. Was he thinking about how their family had cleared the land themselves? Every handful of earth represented hours of toil. They'd cut down trees and removing stumps. The field was a matter a pride for every family member.

The family honor—that's what he was surely thinking about. Somehow, he believed that this quest would preserve it.

27

"If I take the sleigh," he said, "I can sing down enough snow to travel by. That will be much faster than riding the horse, and I'll be able to carry more supplies." He looked at his family again. "Please understand. I go to bring honor to our family name."

He yanked the barn door handle, but Aino cried out from a sudden sense of danger. This would be her last chance to prevent something terrible. "Don't!"

Her mother stared at her. "Hush, child," she said with a swat at Aino's shoulder. "I'm the last person to say your brother should go make a fool of himself in front of Vane, but I won't cry at the top of my lungs about it so neighbors three farms away can hear. If Jouko insists on being a fool, we cannot stop him."

Aino had done her best to coax and plead, but the time for stronger measures had come. "Something bad will happen. I don't know what, but it will be terrible. Maybe you'll be hurt in the dark. The sleigh could crash into a tree, or you'll be too tired to sing enough snow. Or it could melt too fast. Or you could make too *much* snow, or slide into a river, or—" She bit her lip and wished she'd swallowed her words before they came out. Doubting her brother's ability to sing well enough to control his sleigh would not convince him to stay. Rather, the opposite.

She was silent on the concern her parents had mentioned and the one she feared most: that Vane would sing her brother to his death.

"Listen to your sister," Mama said. "Travel in the dark can be dangerous." She clucked her tongue. "Son, why not wait a few weeks, when it's closer to Midsummer Night? Then you can travel well into the evening with have plenty of light."

Midsummer was weeks away, yet if they managed to get him to wait that long, perhaps the urge to duel Vane would ebb by then. And if not, at least he'd travel more safely; at Midsummer, the night was never dark; the sun circled the sky instead of rising and setting.

"I go tonight."

Day and night were equal now—the days had far more sunlight than there had been not long ago in the dead of winter.

"But every week brings more light," Mama said.

Jouko took her by one shoulder and Aino by the other. "Trust me; I'll soon return as victor. I'm the best singer either of you has ever heard, am I not?" He tried to smile away their concerns.

With a sad nod, Aino agreed. "You are the best wizard I have ever heard."

But I've never heard Vane sing. For that matter, she'd never heard anyone outside of Marjala. Tears leaked from her eyes and trickled down her cheeks.

Ever since she'd seen Vane in the marketplace, ever since he bought her the fox pelt—which would remain hidden forever if she had her way—the dread had never left her. The weight felt like a pail of granite rocks, and every day another stone was added.

Pleased with Aino's response, Jouko turned to Mama, who hadn't answered. He posed the question again. "I *am* the best singer you've ever heard, aren't I?"

Her lips turned down, and her chin quaked. "Don't go."

Anger flashed across his face at the sidestep. He shook his head as color rose in his cheeks. He looked around the room again—at Aino, Mama, Sanna, Papa.

"I *am* going," he said. "You cannot stop me."

"Think of *us*." Mama wailed. "We will be the laughing stock of the village!"

They'd all tried to dissuade him, but he was determined—that was clear. Aino could think of naught to do or say that would change his mind, so instead she went up to her toes and hugged him hard. "Be safe."

He hugged her in return, and after she pulled away, Aino untied one of her braids. It tumbled to her shoulder, and she held out the length of red ribbon. "Take this with you. When you look at my ribbon, think of me. Remember that I am waiting for you. This ribbon is not a gift. You must return it to me." She placed it into his palm and curled his fingers around it. "Do whatever you must to return my ribbon to me."

Jouko's mouth softened from its hard line. He opened his hand to look at the ribbon. Gently, he tied it to the top buttonhole of his blue coat. "I'll keep it close to me. And I *will* return it to you the moment I come home."

29

Aino nodded, her emotions so close to the surface that she didn't trust her voice to say more than a few words. She threw her arms around his neck again. "Sing your best, brother."

"I will, sweet sister," he whispered in her ear. He pulled back and looked over the family one last time. "I hope that one day you'll understand why I must do this." He took Aino's hands in his. "I *will* return. No old man—reliable or not—will best me."

Aino nodded and wiped tears from her cheeks. Jouko pulled the stable door open and went inside. Aino dropped onto a nearby stone and covered her face, tears wetting her apron.

She'd be unable to sleep or eat until Jouko returned. She would not be well until she knew that her premonition had been a maid's silly fancy.

The family stayed by the stable door for several minutes despite the chill of the evening. Inside, they heard Jouko hitching up his horse to the sleigh. He sang to aid the preparations. His low, sonorous voice came through the wooden boards of the stable walls.

What if he is good enough to best Vane? He could be, Aino thought hopefully. The stable door opened, and Jouko's tune and words shifted. At the stable door, snowflakes fluttered from the cloudless sky. When enough had fallen, the sleigh pulled out.

Jouko was bundled with mittens and a hat, neither of which he'd brought with him to the stables. He'd probably made them out of other objects inside the stable. The realization that he could protect himself from the cold was strangely comforting.

He'll be fine, Aino reassured herself as he pulled away from the farm.

Slowly, his form disappeared into the thick woods as he followed a path of white ahead of him, just wide enough for his sleigh. He turned briefly to face them, smiled broadly, and waved.

Aino tried to wave back with similar enthusiasm, but her arm felt like wilted birch bark. By the time the sleigh was out of sight, tears stained her cheeks once more, and her limbs shook with both cold and fear.

Win, dear brother. Come home to us.

Chapter Four

Singing down snow from the cloudless sky, Jouko drove his sleigh through a grove of birch. The buds of pale leaves budded with the promise of life, past deep green pines that rose to the sky like fingers reaching for the gods.

He maneuvered around a bend and had to slow down to make way for a group of merchants pulling their wagons back to their villages from another marketplace. As they saw him, their faces showed both awe and disappointment—the former because they witnessed magic right in front of them, and the latter because they would have to tromp through snow, though winter had passed.

Jouko nodded at the group, still singing as he glided along. He went over ferns and around wild blueberry patches, having no trouble singing down just the right amount of snow for the sleigh's runners to glide across the ground in spite of the warm weather. He took every journey by sleigh, regardless of the season, so he had plenty of practice with snow. Over the years, he'd experimented with melodies, cadences, and even the words of power that condensed and cooled the air, making the perfect snow for the runners to skim across.

And, until Vane had shown up at the Marjala town market, Jouko had been certain that *he* was the most powerful wizard. *He* had the townspeople's admiration and respect. His was the magic they turned to when a plow bent, a horse broke a leg, a roof leaked.

If I don't win this duel, instead of the village wizard, I will be the village fool.

The reminder increased the tempo of his charm. He sang with more intent, eager to reach the knoll where Vane made his home. With luck, he'd find the hidden dwelling even if it had repellant and camouflage spells on it.

The faster Jouko sang, the faster the snow fell, and the faster the sleigh could travel. He repeated the six-note melody, an eye on sinking sun all the while. The days stretched longer than they had been only weeks ago, as winter gradually released its hold on the land. Yet he still wished for a few more hours of daylight. Too bad Vane hadn't come in a few more weeks, closer to Juhannus—Midsummer Night, when the sun shone all night instead.

I can't wait until Juhannus. If I don't save my reputation soon, it will be but vapor by then.

Hours of song began to take their toll. Despite the crisp air on his nose and cheeks, Jouko's forehead beaded with sweat from the exertion of maintaining magic for so long, and his voice started to crack here and there on the higher notes. He took off his wool cap and placed it on the bench beside him. Perhaps that would cool him down. Another deep breath for the next rhythm, then a flick of the reins so his honey-colored horse would pick up her pace yet again.

He'd brought the faster of his two horses instead of the stronger one, but with no idea what type of terrain lay ahead, he didn't yet know if he'd made a wise decision.

The narrow path he'd followed southward gradually widened into a broad, highly traveled road flanked by more thick forest with a variety of trees and shrubs—shades of green and brown as far as he could see.

As time wore on, he passed fewer and fewer merchants, whose carts were responsible for the deep ruts cut into the road. Jouko directed extra snow into the ruts so the sleigh wouldn't sink into them and topple.

When almost an hour had passed since the last sign of anyone else on the road to slow him down, Jouko whistled to his horse to speed up. Soon he was practically flying through the woods, sometimes skidding around bends. The sleigh narrowly missed a tree after tree, boulder after boulder. Had his mother been there, she'd have been sure of his imminent death. But appearances aside, Jouko was in full control of the sled and the snow.

Out of the corner of his eye, he spotted a bear running through the trees, thin and surely hungry after a long winter's sleep. In surprise, Jouko's voice skipped a note. Only one, but alas, the most important.

The thick white flakes stopped for the less than the space of a breath, but that was enough for the sleigh to hit a patch of dirt and stone. The force jolted Jouko forward; his horse bucked and whinnied. He clung to the reins as the sleigh skidded on the dry forest road and threatened to crash into a patch of pines and mountain ash.

He inhaled as fast as he could and renewed his song—louder, with more complex words and runs, thickening the snow on his left. He created a bank just in time; instead of crashing into the trees, the sleigh curved to right and returned solidly to the road.

Jouko's hands began to shake. He pulled the reins and called for the horse to stop. When all was still, he pressed the back of his hand to his mouth, feeling the stuttered breath. He needed several moments to regain his wits after such a narrow escape.

After a time, he cleared his throat in preparation to test his strength. For a moment, he considered heading back home. But then he remembered the villagers. How powerful they believed Vane must be. How they wished Marjala had such a wizard.

They already do have such a wizard. I cannot go home, not yet. I shall go on, and I shall beat him. I shall prove my strength in magic.

He drew in another deep breath and let out a low, rumbling tone. As his mind cleared and his nerves settled, he worked the charm deliberately and slowly. The horse shook its mane, snorted, and settled into a trot as if nothing untoward had happened. Jouko smiled inside, relieved. Death from a duel with Vane would be one thing—something Jouko had no intention of experiencing—but to think he could have died before the challenge? That was unbearable.

Jouko's song was quieter than before; he was still somewhat out of breath, but he also sang extra carefully. Better to travel a little more slowly than to go too fast and have your progress halted altogether. He hit every note, enunciated each syllable. With deliberate intent, he focused on the path before him and guided the snow to the curves in the road ahead. Once again, the sleigh swished through the trees.

Sing I snow, of white and frost.
Falling fast before my mare
Gently rest upon the ground
As horse and runners fly.

By the time he'd fully regained his breath capacity, the road had straightened and stretched before him like a long ribbon of honey candy, with no curves to maneuver around. Tall trees lined the way like a giant corridor. He could race through this section of the forest. Jouko picked up the tempo.

For a moment, he thought he heard sleigh bells in the distance. He must have imagined the sound. He hadn't seen a soul in two leagues at least, and the sun had set. No one else would ride at this hour, let alone a fellow wizard. Only the finest wizards could do travel as he did.

Jouko concentrated so hard on pitch and rhythm that he didn't notice a crossroads ahead—or the sleigh barreling from the right—until it was upon him. Both Jouko and the other driver on his sleigh skidded and turned. Their horses veered with sharp curves to avoid the inevitable. All they got for their efforts was the sleighs slamming into each other. The sound of splintered wood made a sickening crunch as Jouko's sleigh collided with the other. Metal twisted. Splinters flew in all directions.

The song fled from Jouko's mind completely. Instead, a yelp of surprise ripped from his throat. Both horses pulled against their lines, which were hopelessly tangled. The animals whinnied in protest as the sleighs pulled them one way and then the other, out of control. Both drivers pulled on their reins, calmed their horses.

Finally, all was still.

Jouko gripped the reins with shaky hands. The harnesses of the two sleighs were in tangles, the sides bent, the runners contorted. He sucked air in great gasps. His heart hammered with dread.

"Reckless boy, rushing on like that," the other driver growled as he clambered to the ground from his own damaged sleigh. The glittering snow squeaked under the man's boots with each step. Jouko shook himself from the shock and forced himself to think through what had just occurred.

The other driver must be a singer too, he realized.

Jouko peered to the right, down the crossroad in the direction the bearded man had come. A thin, even line of snow wound into the horizon like a perfect silver thread—silvery and perfect. The only things marring it were the tracks of the horse's hooves and lines the runners left behind. The snow sparkled like diamonds against the last of day's light. Under other circumstances, he would have admired such magic. Now, he could only compare it with his own and see where his fell short.

He looked back at his own white trail, at the snow he'd been so proud of. In comparison to the old man's, it looked uneven, with lumps and pits. Instead of catching any light, his snow was dull and gray. Envy and self-doubt crept into Jouko's chest.

The other driver studied his bent runners and shook his head, a long beard moving side to side like a pendulum. "Look what you did." He threw his arms into the air in frustration. "The shaft-bows are bent, the hames are wrecked. My sleigh might as well be kindling. Tell me who you are, you stupid, stupid boy, so I know who to sing a curse onto." The collar of his fur coat was turned up and covered his face to his cheeks, but his eyes were clearly visible, steely and intense.

The difference in their snow trails suddenly didn't matter, not when he needed to continue his quest—and escape this madman.

But who *was* this old man who sang such perfect snow and then belittled a fellow wizard? Clearly their trails varied in quality, but Jouko had other songs more powerful than making snow. Who was this man to show such disrespect to a singer of Jouko's caliber? Besides, he'd been tired and distracted after a long day's journey. Surely his first snow of the day had looked as pristine as the old man's.

With as much bravado as he could muster, Jouko stepped forward. "And exactly who do you think *you* are?" he demanded of the other, who had turned back to his sleigh.

As the man crouched, only his brown fur coat was visible. He checked the damage to a runner and groaned with irritation.

Jouko spoke louder to get his attention and demand his respect. "I am Jouko, the singer in the village of Marjala. I'm on an important trip, which your careless driving has interrupted. Who are *you* that you think you can rush headlong through the woods, you miserable old man?"

Slowly, the object of his anger straightened. He turned about at the same even pace, his deep-set eyes boring into Jouko's. "Who am *I*?" His gravelly voice rumbled through his barrel-shaped chest. The man clearly had strength that belied his years. Judging by the breadth of his coat, his arms had to be thick with muscles. He exuded an aura of power, gray beard and deep wrinkles in his forehead notwithstanding.

Something tugged at Jouko's memory. His mouth went dry. *It can't be. Oh, skies, no.*

"Who am I?" The man pulled off his red woolen hat and folded down his collar. He jutted lifted his chin and enunciated each word. "I am Vane. Perhaps you've heard of me?" His mouth turned up in a quirk on one side as if he found the situation humorous. Jouko had heard of Vane; who hadn't? The entire land knew of the wizard at the center of this very journey.

Jouko's voice—usually deep and ready to sing—caught in his throat. "You—you are V—Vane?" How had he not recognized the very person he'd set out to find?

Vane put his fists on his hips, spreading his coat to the sides, which revealed the pouch at his belt. There was the red Braid of Fate and the famed knife with the handle made of reindeer antler. No mistake, this was Vane himself.

I'm not ready. He was supposed to be the one surprised. Jouko again compared their snow trails—and shivered. Perhaps Vane *was* the better singer. But no. Snow wasn't Jouko's only charm; it was simply a complicated one he used often. But he'd mastered many other, stronger, charms.

And this is my only chance to use them. Challenge him. Now. Jouko stood his ground, pulling his shoulders back. He opened his mouth to utter the challenge, but Vane interrupted.

"Move, boy." He waved Jouko away. "I've no use for the likes of you. I must fix the damage you caused and be on my way. I have things to do. Besides, a young tyke should make way for his elders." Without a response, Vane again turned his back to Jouko and sang in a rumbling voice. One of the twisted metal runners untwisted, straightened, and smoothed out until it looked new.

Boy? Young tyke? Jouko cared nothing for how quickly and flawlessly the man's sleigh was repaired. Fury burned in his chest. He stood with his boots far apart, his hands on his own belt to show off his knife. He stood as tall as he could.

"I am younger than you," he said, "but age does not bestow wits or magical strength."

Vane's song paused mid-phrase, which sent a piece of metal half untwisted, to the ground. He eyed it with annoyance and glared at Jouko. "What are you suggesting, *child?*" He stressed the last word as if intentionally lobbing an insult.

I succeed or fail here and now.

He jutted his chin forward. "I will not make way for you, old man. Let the better, stronger singer have the road to himself."

Vane faced Jouko fully, mouth quirked with amusement. "Really, *boy?* And what could you know about strength or wits or memory . . . or magic? You can make snow, I see, but that's hardly impressive. Even a two-year apprentice can do that."

On the contrary, Jouko knew of no apprentice, two-year or otherwise, who could sing snow, and precious few wizards who could. Yet this man viewed such a power as simple?

"Hmm. I suppose you see me as a weak, old man." He sauntered closer with the energy of a boy, gesturing broadly with trunk-like arms. "Who am I, that I should know magic, when I've spent my days alone, with only fields to look at and cuckoo birds to listen to. Is that what you think?"

"N-no. No, of course not." Jouko felt himself take an unintentional step backward.

The closer Vane drew, the more threatening his voice became. Jouko's chest and throat tightened. He refused to step away again, but he couldn't help but lean back slightly. His feet wanted to move, but he focused on keeping them planted on the mossy ground. He would not yield.

Fate has brought me here. I'll never find him again. I will stay, and I will defeat him.

Vane leaned in so close that their noses nearly touched and a few bristly whiskers brushed Jouko's chin. "What makes you think you're so powerful? Why are you better than all the others I've encountered? You, a mere boy?"

Jouko gulped, or tried to; his mouth had dried up as if it were filled with salt. "I'm *not* a child." With the declaration, he allowed himself to step back. He needed space to defy Vane and show his strength. "I know more than you assume, for certain. You see, I was trained by the great Seppo." He opened his arms wide in an invitation. "Therefore, I challenge you. Wit to wit, song to song. We'll see who the greater wizard is."

With a sigh that sounded almost like boredom, old Vane shook his head. "Don't waste my time, foolish boy. You've already made me late. You don't frighten me, if that's what you're trying to do. No song, no spell of yours could possibly scare me."

"But—"

"Let me be," Vane said, his tone now clipped. "I have a sleigh to fix." The old man grunted disdainfully and returned to his repairs, using low vibrations. The bent sides rippled like water then smoothed until they were as flat as the surface of a windless lake.

The speed and accuracy of the spell impressed Jouko. *I cannot allow myself to be distracted. Think!* He narrowed his eyes, going through dozens of songs in his head. Which should he start with? He took several large steps, grabbed Vane's shoulder, and whirled him about to face him. The old man's song cut off.

"He who refuses to stand when he's challenged is no better than a pig," Jouko declared. The moment the words left his mouth, he nearly gasped and apologized for them. Had he truly called Old Reliable Vane *a pig*? Had he completely lost his senses?

"A pig, you say?" Vane arched a bushy eyebrow. "You think so?"

"Yes." Jouko balled his fists to feel more powerful. "A pig."

"Careful, boy," Vane said. "Didn't Seppo teach you that spoken words have power?"

"Of course he did," Jouko shot back. He'd see this duel through to the end. His future—his family's reputation, along with untold possible wealth—hinged on this moment. "I said you're a pig, and I meant it. Watch me give you a snout and a curly tail."

The more he spoke, the hotter the fury in his belly grew. He found himself speaking threats without thinking through them. But Vane's reminder about words didn't stop Jouko.

"After you're squealing on the ground, I'll knock you about, into trees and down again, rolling across the country-side. And when at last you're dead, I'll toss your body onto a dunghill in the corner of a cowshed."

Finished, Jouko stood there, his breathing heavy as he waited for his opponent's response.

Vane laughed.

The sound seemed to puncture Jouko's chest with a bitter blade.

With the back of one hand, Vane touched one eye as if wiping away tears of mirth, but then calmly raised a sausage-like finger and spoke evenly, seriously. "Only a fool threatens Vane."

Jouko had but a moment to consider what the man meant before Vane raised his arms to the sides and inhaled, filling his chest with air. Before the man could sing, Jouko tried to take a deep breath of his own. But all of his songs had fled his mind. He could not think of so much as a note to begin with.

A pig. He'd been about to sing Vane into a pig. Could he *unsing* that kind of enchantment? Not that Jouko would want to.

The old man's cracked voice made way for a sonorous note that burst forth with magic. That single tone conjured power so intense, Jouko felt it to his toes. As Vane sang, he concentrated, which deepened the heavy lines in his forehead until they looked like furrows in a field. The song felt dark, oppressive.

Nothing, of course, like Jouko's first-year songs he learned with Seppo, which had been full of cheer and childlike laughter.

This was a level of magic he never knew existed. It pulled him downward and pressed on his chest, making each breath an effort. The ground vibrated beneath his feet. Branches above them quaked as if they, too, feared Vane. Even hills in the distance seemed to quiver. A nearby stream left its course on the way to a small pond and suddenly jumped its banks, splashing every which way. Was the water drawn to Vane, or fleeing from him?

Stones at the shore split in two; with horrible cracks of what sounded like thunder, fallen logs split in half. Jouko wanted to press his palms to his ears to keep out the cacophony, to close his eyes so he couldn't see the world about him shake at the rhythms and words from Vane.

But Jouko did not cover his ears or close his eyes. He stood still as a stone, not because he was brave or trying to show that he had no fear, but rather because he *couldn't* move. Had a wave of his hand been all it took to win the duel, Jouko still wouldn't have been able to move.

The song changed to higher, quicker notes. Jouko's eyes widened as his own sleigh changed—but not in the way Vane had fixed his own. The runners sprouted saplings, and the bench turned into a willow bush. The sleigh lifted from the ground as lightly as a bird and drifted toward the pond.

Jouko tried to raise a hand in protest, but still his body refused to obey any command.

He couldn't sing, but he could speak a little. "Stop," he managed breathily. "Don't!"

The man didn't heed him but continued to carry the sleigh farther away. It floated closer and closer to the pond. Desperate to save his sleigh, Jouko searched his memory for a spell.

The song of return. Relieved to have remembered something at last, Jouko opened his mouth but barely a squeak of the tune emerged. The sleigh continued its flight.

The song to catch what falls. Quick!

He conjured the words, but in his haste, his pitch was off. The sleigh floated onward. When it reached the middle of the pond, it tilted slowly then hung suspended in the air for a moment before it landed with a crash in the center of the pond with an enormous splash.

Jouko's mind whirled, grasped at memories of lessons he'd studied with Seppo. His teacher had once been as powerful as Vane. Surely Seppo had taught something that could defeat the old man.

So why has every powerful charm fled me? Breathless, Jouko gasped out a simple song—one that brought to the owner a lost object.

Again, failure. By now, his voice rasped—and rose no louder than a whisper. All he could do was stammer, "My—my sleigh!"

The man had done far more than destroy the runners and dunk the sleigh into the water. He'd also made Jouko powerless to stop it. He'd watched it all, unable to move, weak as a newborn kitten.

Vane's song continued, with words and progressions Jouko could never have imagined. The magic resonated deeply. He could almost see the magic as otherworldly colors that swirled all around the two men.

Without warning, Jouko's woolen scarf untied itself and drifted into the sky—fast enough that it slipped out of reach as he grasped for it. He watched, head back, as his dingy yellow scarf went higher and higher, finally settling into the sky, where it looked like an uneven storm cloud.

"M-my—" He raised a hand to point at his scarf in the sky, only to see his mitten slip off his hand and tumble around and around into the air. He tried to snatch it, but his other mitten slipped off as well. The pair seemed to dance in the air high above his head, twirling this way and that until they suddenly flew off toward the pond, where they spun in place and then dropped where the sleigh had sunk moments before. They scarcely disturbed the smooth surface of the water.

Somehow Jouko's blue coat came off—how or when he did not know, only that it drifted up, up, up, and found a home in the sky as his scarf had. The dark blue of his coat made for a deep smudge in the paler blue of the sky. Shouldn't the sky be darker now, with the sun about to set? Perhaps Vane's magic could control time as well.

High above him in the sky, Jouko noted a small red splotch on one end of what used to be his coat. *Aino's ribbon.* Her voice from their farewell returned to his mind. *Take this with you. When you look at my ribbon, think of me. Remember that I am waiting for you. This ribbon is not a gift. You must return it to me.*

"I promised to return," he whispered, needing to hear the promise aloud. "I must go home. I must."

He felt himself drawn toward the pond, pulled by magic. If he didn't act soon, he'd wind up drowned in the water at Vane's hand.

With Aino and her ribbon in mind, Jouko bellowed, "Enough!"

The cry was enough to make Vane's song waver the slightest bit, a gap in song just long enough for a skilled singer to take the advantage. Jouko did just that. He created a thick barrier of air that would keep him safe from the pond. He prayed to the gods that he'd soon be able to go on the attack rather than remain in a defensive stance. A song from a position of strength would be the only way to gain the upper hand and end this duel.

When Vane's song no longer dragged Jouko toward the pond, he responded not with annoyance or frustration, but simply with a vicious gleam in his eye. He didn't stop singing, but the song changed. Vane used new words and increased his volume, all the while staring at Jouko as if he could see beneath one's skin.

Attack him, Jouko ordered himself. *Sing!* He drew in breath, but his lungs were only half full when his windpipe felt as if a hand were clamped about it. He'd trained for difficult moments, though never one like this. *You are a wizard. Defend yourself.*

But no matter what he tried, Jouko couldn't get one note past his lips.

And Vane sang on.

Wetness seeped into Jouko's boots. He looked down to find his feet sinking into thick mud. This patch of soil hadn't been swampy before; this was Vane's magic. Jouko tried to step out of it, but the mud was thick as pitch and his feet as heavy as granite blocks. Slowly, he began to sink, first past the toes of his boots. Then deeper, deeper. His feet disappeared to the ankles.

Jouko again strained to pull one foot and then the other from the muck, to no avail. He reached down and tried to pull on his boot with his hand, but that had no effect either.

"Old Reliable Vane," he said with the utmost in respect, which he should have shown right away, alas, "You *are* the greatest singer the world has ever known. I confess it."

In response, the wizard gave Jouko a nod of acknowledgment, but he kept singing. The muddy area widened and thickened. And Jouko kept was sucked in further.

"Sir. Old Reliable. Free me. Please." No use pretending that he felt no terror.

Vane's dark song went on and on, its slow tempo as maddening as it was unnerving. Slowly, inevitably, Jouko sank into the ground until the mud reached the middle of his thighs.

"Reverse your charms," Jouko pled. "I beg of you!"

If Vane were to repeat his curses backward, the spells would be reversed. Few wizards were adept at such reversals, but if anyone could do it, surely that person was Vane.

"I'll pay you. Take any of my possessions," Jouko said. His words came in bursts as he fought for air. "Whatever you want. Please."

At that, Vane's song faded away. He stepped over to a birch tree and absently peeled off some bark. "What do you have to offer?"

Jouko didn't dare consider the question a sign that he'd escape this mess. Instead, he frantically thought through his most valuable possessions. "I have two of the best crossbows ever created. The first shoots arrows faster than the eye can see. The other is the most accurate bow in the land. It can hit a coin at the end of a field with hardly any effort. Take either one."

Vane sang a triplet, and the viselike tightness around his throat lessened ever so slightly. Jouko's hands went to his neck, and he breathed in precious cool air.

"I don't want a crossbow," Vane said dismissively. "I have plenty of my own." He took another deep breath, sang again, notes that descended—down, down.

In time with the music, the swampy ground sucked Jouko in further, until the mire reached his waist. Vane let the song hang in the air before cutting it off.

Fear coursed through Jouko's body. He pressed his hands against the ground on either side of him and pushed as hard as he could to lift himself out. His body didn't budge so much as the width of a pine needle.

Vane stepped away from the birch and clasped his hands behind his back as he walked in a circle around Jouko. "What else do you have to offer? Or shall we get this over with now?"

"No! I have more." Jouko stopped his struggle and lifted his face to Vane, who had one hairy eyebrow raised in mild curiosity. "I have two of the handsomest boats you've ever seen. One can win any race."

With a roll of his eyes, Vane sang again. Once more, Jouko felt himself sinking. The mud reached his ribs and pressed on his chest. He had to take shallow breath to speak—he could not have held a note no matter how hard he tried.

"My other boat is strong!" Jouko spoke more quickly. He had to get words out as fast as he could, before Vane sang him to death. "It holds safe any cargo you ask of it. Say the word, and either boat is yours." Another set of breaths, then, "Or both! They can both be yours. Just free me; I beg of you."

Once again Vane's song stopped. He kept walking around Jouko, one eye on him as if he were a piece of livestock to be bartered on. Vane didn't resume his song, at least for the moment.

Jouko breathed a sigh of shaky relief. The more he could keep Vane talking, the better. But how long would that work? And what did Jouko have that would any appeal to Vane?

The old man looked down at him as one would a child about to poke a sleeping bear. "I have many boats already, at least one at nearly every river and lake between here and the North Country. I assumed you'd heard about me."

"I have, but—I—"

Vane took up the dark song again. Once more, the descending notes pushed Jouko deeper into the ground. The sludge pinned his arms to his sides. His torso began to slip beneath the surface.

"My horses!" he yelled in desperation. "The one here is fast. The other is strong. Take them. Just reverse the spell." His voice had lost any trace of confidence or bravado, but he didn't care; he had to beg for his life. His swampy prison pressed against his chest; he could hardly get any air at all.

By the irritated look on Vane's face, his interest in horses was no greater than it was in crossbows or boats.

What I would give to sing one last time. Jouko's consciousness began to fade. At any moment, he'd faint away. His foolish ego had brought him here, and now he would die, unable to sing at the end. Yet even that one joy was lost to him.

Without any real hope that his offer would be accepted, Jouko offered all the gold he possessed. Again, Vane turned him down. Why wouldn't he? A man as wealthy as Vane would want no meager bag of coins or ought else someone as lowly as Jouko had to offer.

The mud reached his shoulders. His neck. His chin. He lifted his face to the sky in an effort to breathe as long as possible.

Above him, the red blotch in the sky drew his eyes. Aino's ribbon.

This ribbon is not a gift. You must return it to me.

How? If he didn't find a way soon, he'd be a dead man, as Aino had feared. He gazed at the mark of her ribbon above him and knew he had one last offer to make.

Skies, let her forgive me.

Hopefully she would understand that it was the only way for him to keep his promise. Hadn't she begged him to do whatever was required to come home alive? Yes, they'd both assumed that keeping such a promise meant using his magic and wit, even if it meant trickery. But not this.

Forgive me, Aino.

"Venerable Vane!" Jouko gasped as his ears filled with mud.

The old wizard had lost what little interest he'd had. He sat on a rock and cleaned his fingernails with his knife. He still sang, but the charm lacked the power it had originally possessed. The ground sucked at him more slowly, but it sent him as surely as ever to his death.

"Vane, hear me. I have one more offer for you."

46

The wizard's only response was a grunt, but his song did stop for the moment.

"I have something I *know* you'd want."

Jouko's tone must have sounded different, for Vane's head came up at that. "You're certain this time?"

He tried to nod. "I'm sure. Please reverse your spell." The pressure around his chest made blood pound in his head. His neck ached from the awkward angle, and he still felt light-headed. He expected to see stars in his vision soon.

Vane stood from the rock and strolled over. He bent down in front of Jouko. "Speak up then." He gestured at him with the point of his knife. "What's your final offer?"

"My sister. My mother's darling. Aino." He took a couple of breaths to get enough air to continue. "She can be your prize, your wife. She'll—she'll sweep your floors, weave your fabrics, bake your bread, and keep you warm at night." He looked up at the ribbon in the sky. Vane followed his gaze.

"See that red spot?" Jouko asked. "That is her ribbon. She gave it to me before I left home. She made me promise to return it to her, no matter the cost."

"I see . . ." The wizard tucked his knife away and stroked his beard again. He did not resume his song, and did not reject the offer out of hand.

"Aino is faithful and true," Jouko said earnestly as a tiny spark of hope ignited inside him. "And she's a very. Good. Cook." The speech had taken the last drop of strength he had; Jouko lapsed into silence and awaited his verdict.

"This sister of yours. . ." Vane pressed his chapped lips together as if in consideration. "Was she at the market in Marjala two days past?"

"Yes!" The spark in Jouko's chest grew into a flame. "Yes, she told me that she was at the fur trader's booth with our mother, when you arrived."

The bushy eyebrows rose. "Red braids tied with ribbons? Green ribbons that day, if I'm not mistaken?"

"Yes!" If the mud hadn't held Jouko captive, his knees would have given way. He wasn't yet saved, but the wizard was softening.

"The girl did catch my eye." Vane rubbed his hands together. "Now *that* is a worthy offer."

Without another word, he started a new song that would create a contract between them. When complete, the agreement would be stronger than if they'd carved it into granite. At the needed times, Jouko joined in, gasping out the words and notes as best he could as he promised his sister to the old man. Vane finished by accepting the offer and renewing the oath between them.

As the final note hung in the air, Jouko waited expectantly. He stared at the only spot he could see clearly—the sky with the darker blue patch that had once been his coat, and the red spot that marked Aino's ribbon. He waited impatiently to be freed. Never again would he take for granted the ability to take a full breath and sing loud and strong.

"I'm a man of my word," Vane said. "Let's get you out."

His voice remained as strong as ever. But this time, the tune and words sounded strange, because the song was simply the original curse in reverse, note for note, syllable for syllable, all backward.

Jouko couldn't understand the words, but that mattered not at all, not when he was slowly—but oh, what bliss!—rising from the ground. First his face was free, and clean as if dirt of any kind had never touched his cheeks. Then his shoulders and chest emerged. He breathed in huge gulps of fresh spring air.

Then he could move his arms. After a few more seconds, he pulled one foot out of the mud, stepping free of his prison—delicious liberty—and then the other. With each, the mire disappeared the moment he stepped onto dry ground. Even his clothes were clean, with not a speck of mud.

A sudden wind blew through the woods, and with it came his scarf, mittens, and coat. They fluttered from the sky and returned to him. He plucked his coat from the air and slipped his arms through each sleeve, then did the same with his scarf and mittens, never happier to wrap the former around his neck or put the latter onto his hands.

His sleigh rose from the pond, and when it returned to the road near him, it had perfectly shaped runners and shiny new paint.

Emotions—joy, relief, wonder—flooded through Jouko in such a rush that he could scarcely bear them all. He dropped to his knees before the wizard. "Thank you, thank you, wise one!"

"I did this only because of your pretty sister." Vane climbed onto his sleigh again and took hold of the reins. "I need someone to care for me and, as you put it"—he grinned lasciviously—"to keep me warm at night. I'll come to claim my prize soon enough."

With his booming voice—a sound Jouko would forever remember—Vane sang snow. He flicked the reins and swished along the road into the forest over a fresh layer of whiteness.

Jouko's strength left him. He made his way to a rock and sat there, panting. His entire body trembled like limp saplings in a storm. He fingered Aino's ribbon, once more tied to the buttonhole of his coat, no longer part of the sky.

Aino. Oh, Aino. He glanced up where it had been as the reality of what had transpired settled in his mind and grew clear. *I've done something horrible.*

Sentencing his sister to a life with Vane wasn't what she meant when she'd insisted he find a way to come home. Yet in the moment, he'd convinced himself otherwise. How could he have let himself be so selfish as to think that his sister would approve of such a bargain?

He pushed himself to his feet and shakily climbed onto his sleigh. He sat there, uneasy, and tried to calm his mind. At last he found the strength to sing. He turned horse and sleigh about and headed toward home.

For an hour, he drove furiously, until he was sure he was alone, that the old man was far away. Then he slowed to a stop near a grove of thick trees where he could be hidden from the main road. There he unhitched the horse. There he'd stay in the woods, at least for one night, until he could find a way to go home and tell his family what he'd done.

Until he could face the shame of telling Aino.

He made a simple campsite then found a brook of fish to catch for dinner. After arranging rocks into a fire pit, he piled kindling and soon had a fire with which to cook his meal. He sat on a stump and cooked the fish over hot coals. His stomach protested with hunger, but he wouldn't sing to speed things along.

A simple melody would have made starting the fire easier. Another would have cooked the fish faster. But he couldn't sing. Awash in guilt, he couldn't utter a note.

Look what I did with magic—I sacrificed my sister's life to save my own.

For her, marriage to Vane would be a fate little better than death.

Jouko's eyes were pulled again and again to the buttonhole with Aino's red ribbon. He tugged one end of the ribbon, releasing the bow. He threaded the fabric through his fingers and wished for a song that could undo the contract and set his sister free.

But he knew of no such song.

So, he made a new vow: he would never sing again unless it meant making Aino free.

Chapter Five

Aino hurried through the forest path to Paavo's home, clutching a sack of coins. Mama had asked one of the girls to purchase leather for Papa's new hat, and before Sanna could say a word, Aino had quickly volunteered to run the errand.

For the three days since Jouko left, the very walls had seeped bitter silence and worry. No one wanted to remain at home, but Aino had a particular reason for wanting leave: to visit Paavo.

To give herself more time with him, she held her skirts up as she ran. She jumped over ferns and wild strawberry bushes, ducked under branches and leapt over decaying logs. With each step, her shoes pressed into the soft, mossy earth.

She arrived at the edge of the Sorsa family's land, breathless, right as Paavo walked out of the shed where the family did their work. When he saw her, his face split into a grin. Aino felt her cheeks flush, and a pleasant flutter came alive in her middle. Paavo checked the house, the clothesline, the woodpile, surely alert for anyone who might discover them. Of most concern, of course, was his mother.

Seeing no one, he crooked a finger and motioned with his head toward a stand of thick pine behind the sauna. She nodded and hurried that direction, her heart hammering against her chest. From exertion, yes, but not entirely.

When the two were hidden from view by pine boughs, Paavo turned around and held out his hands. She placed hers in his, and he squeezed them in his warm, strong grip. "I'm glad you came—I wanted to see you today." Paavo's warm eyes and gentle voice made her trembly all over.

"Me, too." She held him tightly, wondering whether the sudden weakness in her knees would make her topple to the forest floor.

He looked over her shoulder, still on alert for any witnesses. "What brings you here?"

They both knew the real question—how much time did they have before she'd be missed?

"I'm to buy enough leather for a new hat for Papa." She held up the coin pouch. "But Mama went to sell eggs to Mrs. Laurinen, and you know how the two of them can gossip. I have at least thirty minutes." Her smile felt so wide that she wondered if she looked like a child caught in mischief. But she couldn't help her happiness, not when she and Paavo had longer than usual to be together, provided Mr. Sorsa didn't miss his son and order him back to work.

She and Paavo tended to get lucky that way; his father leaned toward forgetfulness and often focused so much on scraping the skins and treating the pelts that he whiled away hours. Some days he practically forgot he had a son unless he came across a chore left undone.

Paavo led her deeper into the woods. "Come here."

Relishing the warmth of his hand, Aino followed through the pines. When they reached a thick oak about a hundred paces from where they began, Paavo turned around. "I want to show you something." His face practically glowed.

"What is it?" Aino looked about her and saw only trees and shrubs, blueberry bushes, and ferns. "And where?"

"Watch." Now Paavo even sounded mischievous. He drew his knife from his belt and walked right up to an older pine with a cracked trunk. With the blade, he seemed about to pry off some bark.

But then a small door flipped open, revealing a hidden cavity within the old tree.

"I'd forgotten all about that," Aino said, delighted. "How did you find it again?"

Years ago, Paavo had fashioned the spot to hide trinkets in. They'd used it as children, and swore each other to secrecy over it. That had been so long ago. Aino almost wished they'd remembered it long ago. The spot would have been perfect for secretly exchanging notes.

"This isn't what I wanted to show you." His voice had turned mysterious.

Aino stepped closer, brow drawn together in curiosity. "Then what is it?" She tried to peer inside, but the shade made seeing into the hole clearly impossible.

Paavo reached inside and drew out a small wooden box. He held it out to her. Aino admired the carvings on top, which she had no doubt Paavo had done himself. With one finger, she traced the delicate lines of two reindeer, one male and one female.

"You," she said, brushing the male reindeer again, "and me?" she finished, settling on the female reindeer.

"Yes." But Paavo didn't sound satisfied.

"How did you—"

"Open it," he interrupted, and held the box out to her. His eyes flashed with excitement.

"All . . . right," she said slowly. What did Paavo have planned?

She slid a wooden peg from the latch and gently lifted the lid. Sunlight filtered through the evergreens all around, casting an emerald light into the box, wherein lay gold and silver coins—so many she couldn't count them at a glance.

"How many—there must be two dozen at least." Eyes wide, Aino looked up. "Where did you get these?"

"I've been saving for over a year." Paavo beamed with pride, clearly pleased with her reaction. "Papa is old. He's agreed to let me have the business next spring. I've been setting my own traps and preparing my own furs long enough that I'm far past an apprentice. He's allowed me to keep any money I earn myself that the family doesn't need. In a few more months, I'll be able to build a house. And in a year, when my father retires, I'll be able to . . ." For likely the first time in Aino's memory, Paavo flushed. His feet shifted below him. The sight made her giddy. He cleared his throat and finished, "I'll be able to support a wife."

He emphasized the last word ever so slightly. He clicked the box closed as it still lay in her hands. Then he licked his lips and waited for her reaction.

Tears of happiness pricked her eyes. She threw her arms around his neck and hugged him tight. "You've done so much, worked so hard for us."

"And?" he prompted. A compliment about his devoted labor wasn't what he wanted, of course.

She released him and looked him in the eye. "And I cannot wait to be your bride."

In but a year, she thought, amazed at the idea. *So soon!* To think that only days ago, she and her mother had discussed whether she was old enough to marry at all.

I must find a way to endear him to Mama. A realization cast a shadow over Aino's joy. *She'll insist on Sanna marrying first.*

Paavo tilted his head to one side and regarded her. "What about your mother?"

"I don't know," Aino said honestly. "Perhaps we'll find a suitor for Sanna. Or we could convince my parents to break the eldest daughter tradition." She wrapped her arms about his waist and pressed her ear to his chest, finding comfort in his heartbeat. "We'll find a way, somehow."

She could imagine no other future for herself than that of Paavo's wife. Yet they both knew that her mother had fantastical dreams of her daughters marrying men of wealth and power. Even if they found an acceptably rich suitor for Sanna, Mama might still insist that Aino was too young, that sisters shouldn't marry so close together. Or she'd find some reason to delay the match in the hope that their interest in each other fade away like a tide. But their love would never fade. They knew that if their parents did not.

Until today, Aino had been patient with the knowledge that they had a difficult journey ahead of them, thinking that they had years to untangle it all. No more. She knew that Paavo was working for their future. He was close to being able to marry.

And now she knew for certain that he indeed wanted her as a wife . . .

"Don't worry about my mother," Aino said with a shake of her head. "We have a year to convince her that you are the man destined to be my husband. We'll find a way, even if we it means a longer wait."

She carefully approached the tree and reverently placed the box back inside it. One day she'd see the box every day. It would grace their mantel. Joy coursed through her, but she had to rein it in rather than dance in celebration and declare their love to the world, which she yearned to do. For now, their plans must remain secret. If her mother were to find out too soon, she'd be liable to burst a blood vessel—then marry Aino to some old widower to prove that *she* was the mother and that no daughter of hers could make such decisions on her own.

Eager and excited all at once, Aino closed the little door, which blended into the trunk again so that she couldn't make out the edges anymore. Paavo slipped his hands about her waist and lifted her off the ground, spinning about. They both laughed, and when he put her back down, her face brushed his.

Paavo softly kissed her cheek, setting her skin afire. Aino looked up at him. Her smile must have been encouragement enough, because he leaned closer and, for the first time, pressed his lips to hers. She clung to him, sure that if she didn't hold tight, she'd float away out of sheer happiness.

When he pulled back, he ran this thumb along her jawline. "I will take good care of you, Aino, I promise."

"I know you will." Her voice was hardly a whisper. "And I wouldn't have anyone else."

"One year from today." Paavo patted the hidden door. "Let's have our wedding be one year from today."

"Yes, let's," Aino said.

No other day could be a more perfect reminder of their first kiss, the first day she saw a glimpse at their future, bright and happy as the eternal sun. She raised herself on her toes and pressed a kiss to his cheek. "I can wait a year to be the wife of Paavo the fur merchant."

He touched one of her braids, which today hung loose, and smoothed his fingers along the surface. "It will be a pity when you must cover your hair."

"You will be worth it," Aino said. She'd do far more for him than wear a kerchief on her head. She'd cut her braids off completely if it meant they could be together the rest of their lives. "And remember, I still have one last year to show off my tresses."

A voice called in the distance. "Paavo? Where are you, son?"

He sighed. "She'll come looking for me if I don't appear right away."

Aino glanced at the sun's angle. "I need to get home soon anyway in case my mother returns early. She's been especially moody the last couple of days and is liable to have a conniption if I'm not there."

For a few minutes, she'd escaped into the happiness of being with Paavo, but now the reason for Mama's irritability returned full force, along with the memory of Jouko on his sleigh. Her brow knit with worry. When would he return? *Would* he return?

His mother's voice pierced the forest walls again. "Paavo? Boy, where are you?"

He put a hand to his mouth and called, "Coming!" But instead of hurrying off, he took Aino by the shoulders. "What's happened?"

"It's Jouko," she said, suddenly emotional.

"What about him?"

She sniffed, glanced in the direction Mrs. Sorsa had called from, and then tried to blink back tears. She looked up at the deep blue sky to keep them from falling. When she trusted herself to speak, she lowered her face and said, "He left to challenge Vane."

Paavo's eyes widened as big as his gold coins in the tree. "He . . . but why?"

"To prove he's the best singer. After Vane's appearance at the market, Jouko could go nowhere without hearing constant comparisons between himself and Old Reliable. He left to challenge him. I wish I knew where he is—and that he's still alive. We've all been so worried."

"Understandably." Paavo's voice was tender, laced with worry of his own. "I will pray to the gods each morn for his safe return."

He took her hand, and the two of them walked back through the woods silently as the weight of her news sank in. As they drew closer to the edge of the clearing where the Sorsa land began, they released hands in unspoken agreement to keep their love a secret for a little longer.

She missed his touch on the instant and wished the secret didn't have to be so. With Jouko away—and possibly worse—who knew when she could reveal their plans to her mother? If things went poorly for Jouko, her mother might not accept any suggestion of an engagement between them for years to come.

At the edge of the trees, Paavo turned and whispered, "I will be buying a betrothal solki soon. Perhaps by then, Jouko will be home. We'll sway your mother, and then we can announce our plans."

"I hope you're right," Aino said. "And I will love any solki you give me." Thanks to his experience in trade, Paavo knew some of the best jewelry makers. The intricately engraved metal brooches were expensive, so women rarely had more than the one given to them by their betrothed. Her mother's solki was silver with an elaborate flower pattern that went around the edge. Biting the corner of her lip with excitement, Aino wondered what hers would look like.

Paavo stepped into the clearing. "Come, Aino," he said loudly for his mother's benefit. "Go inside. I will be right in to show you some pieces that your mother would approve of for your father's hat."

"Why, thank you, Paavo," Aino replied, equally loudly.

He lowered his voice and whispered, "If you can wait a moment while I speak to Mama, I'll walk you to the path and give you a *proper* farewell." He grinned and eyed her lips. Aino's stomach flipped over several times.

"Is that a promise?" she asked, hand on the door.

"One my lips are eager to keep."

Chapter Six

Behind the house, Aino heaved a second rug over the birch frame then wiped her damp forehead. The spring afternoon was still relatively cool, but beating dirt out of rugs made her warm and sticky. She picked up the slapper made of bent saplings and noticed for the first time how much the three-ringed design looked like the Braid of Fate. Her hands gripped the handle, and she whacked harder than she had before.

With each strike, a cloud of dust burst from the rug, which she struck again and again, as it could put her in control of her fate somehow. But no matter how much she whacked the rug—which was well past the point of clean—the image of Vane would not leave her mind. He seemed to dwell in her memory as he'd been when he'd left the market but then turned back and pierced her with his gaze.

At last she changed out the rug for another, and as she beat third one, which was from the room she shared with Sanna, she shoved thoughts of Vane from her mind and tried to think instead of happier things. Of Paavo, and how he'd saved money for their future and wanted to be her husband. Of the thrill of their first kiss.

She dabbed some beads of perspiration from her brow and smoothed back a stray piece of hair that had escaped a braid. Her fingers trailed down the braid to the end and lingered on the blue ribbon tied there. The happiness evaporated like morning dew under the sun, and unease took its place. Red was her favorite color, but she hadn't the heart to wear any since Jouko left—wasn't sure she'd wear red again until after he returned. *If* he returned.

Strange how her intense happiness from a moment before could be so quickly tempered by thoughts of her brother.

No one knew exactly how far south Vane's Knoll stood. And if Jouko did find it, what if Vane wasn't there? If he'd come to Marjala on a whim, he could be traveling elsewhere at any time. For all she knew, Jouko might not be home for weeks, if ever. She hit the rug with all her might. The slapper creaked under the strain. Breathing heavily, she dropped her arms and let it fall to the grass. Could she stand weeks—or more—of this misery?

The worry that had begun to gnaw at her middle when Jouko first mentioned his foolish plan intensified. It overshadowed her happiness and kept her awake at night. The looking glass above the wash basin in her room testified to that, revealing purplish circles beneath her eyes.

Whether milking the cow or simply walking past the fireplace in the main room, she felt detached, as if she didn't belong to the world around her. As if, at any moment, her life would unravel like so much knitting. As if she walked across a newly frozen lake with spots where the ice remained so thin that her weight would crack the surface, sending her into deadly dark water.

The wait for Jouko gnawed at the entire family. At times, a look or a tone from her mother felt not unlike icy water. Her father didn't yell; he sulked in silence, which felt like a suffocating cloak thrown over the home. As for Sanna, she spent hours a day in the corner, knitting furiously as if she could push away the apprehension if only her needles could move fast enough.

For Aino, the rugs had been a welcome distraction, if a brief one. She raised her arm to wipe her face again—one more rug still waited to be beaten—and noticed a movement in the trees—too steady and too big to be bird or squirrel.

Arm still raised, she shielded her eyes from the sun and tried make out what, or who, made the movement. Light and shadow kept shifting. A twig snapped, and another, and then the sound of shrubs brushing against pant legs was suddenly clear. Someone approached—at least one person, but likely more.

Were they coming to visit Mama? Could it be Vane, come victorious after the duel?

Could it be Jouko? No, he'd left with his sleigh. If he were returning, he'd be singing; she'd have heard his approach first.

Then it can't be Vane, either. If the wizard were to come, he'd surely do so by some magical means as well. But she heard no song.

She stepped away from the rug, and the slapper still unheeded to her feet. Shading her eyes, she watched the road leading from their house to the forest. At last, the movement became clear; the blur resolved into a man leading a horse, head down in defeat.

He looked like Jouko, at least from a distance, and the horse certainly looked like his. But if this was her brother, where was the sleigh? And why didn't he sing? If he found Vane and lost the duel, how was he alive? The more she pondered, the more the questions multiplied.

At last the figure stepped from the shadows into the cleared family land. Sunlight broke across his straw-colored hair and illuminated a red ribbon tied to a button hole of his coat. *Her* ribbon.

Jouko! It is Jouko. Relief burst through Aino. She picked up her skirts and ran, both laughing and crying, toward the entry to their farmstead, where her brother still walked, slow step by slow step, his head down.

"You made it!" She kicked up dirt behind her as she ran. "You're back!" She couldn't hold in her happiness. He must have come out of the duel victorious. Mama must have heard her, for the house door opened, and Mama popped her head out.

"Aino, why are you yell—" Her voice caught in a strangled cry as her eyes landed on the shape of Jouko. "My son!" Her hands flew to her mouth.

He looked up at her high-pitched scream and stopped walking. He stood there, holding the horse's lead rope, shoulders rounded. Aino quickly went through a mental list of things he'd surely need—good food, plenty of water, and sleep for days. A bath, surely.

Mama thundered down the steps. Aino heard her footsteps and turned to embrace her mother with joy. They wept

60

together, and when they pulled apart, Aino tugged on her mother's hand. "Let's go greet him."

He yet stood in the same spot as if his feet had grown roots, staring vacantly with empty eyes. Aino wasn't sure he was even aware of their presence. As she they neared, she could make out Jouko's red and splotchy face. He looked as if he'd been crying.

"My boy!" Mama piped up. "You beat Vane, didn't you? I knew you could. You've made your family proud. Stories of your exploits will be passed down from one generation to another, just you wait."

Through her joy, Aino remembered what one of her first thoughts: that her brother wouldn't have returned without his sleigh. Yet here he was, beside his horse, without his sleigh. Her insides twisted.

Something is wrong. Terribly wrong.

Mama threw her arms around his stiff body and sobbed into his chest, wailing that her only son had returned with honor, and that she'd feared the worst.

Jouko didn't respond right away. Indeed, for a moment, Aino wondered if her brother was under an enchantment. Perhaps he did not know who or where he was. But then his eyes welled with tears, and he wiped his nose with a coat sleeve. His body jerked as he tried to hold back emotion. His face tightened with pain, but finally he let out a wail of utter mourning. He looked pale and ready to collapse. He might have traveled for days in a near delirium.

"Let's help him to the bench by the house." Aino gently extracted Jouko from her mother's embrace and encouraged her to slip an arm behind his back so the two women could support him the rest of the way.

After what couldn't have been more than a few minutes but felt like an eternity. Aino had to learn what had transpired over the last several days. Jouko dropped to the old bench, shaking as tears poured down his cheeks.

Aino sat beside him, doing her all to push back the sense of dread that persisted. "You're home now," she told her brother, her hand on his back as he leaned over and covered his face.

With no room for Mama on the bench, she ran off to the field to fetch Papa. He soon appeared, huffing and covered in dirt.

"What is it?" he asked, looking about frantically. "Who's hurt?"

Mama hadn't waited for him. She'd already rushed back to the bench, where she hopped from one foot to the other. Papa drew closer and took in the scene. "Son," he said in a tone more of disbelief than of affection. "You're back."

In answer, Jouko looked up, his face a mask of misery.

Mama dropped to her knees on the grass and looked up at Jouko. "You *are* safe and well, aren't you?" Her words weren't a question, but a demand for confirmation. "What happened? You won, didn't you? You wouldn't be home otherwise. Right? Speak, son. Tell me I'm right."

From the door, Sanna called, "Did you find Vane?"

"Come now," their mother said, ignoring Sanna. "Enough of silence. Tell us every detail." She clasped her hands, set them in her lap, and waited like a young girl expecting a story.

Jouko opened his mouth, but no words came out. He wiped a hand across his face and looked to the side as if to avoid everyone's gaze.

He's alive, Aino told herself. *He doesn't appear injured. And yet . . .*

Perhaps he was simply fatigued. The journey alone had to be taxing, and that didn't account for the exhaustion after a duel. It would be a wonder if he *hadn't* been tired out.

But the sides of his mouth pulled down, and his eyes were glassy. This was not a victorious man.

"Well?" Mama said, her voice impatient, demanding. "*Did* you find Vane?"

Jouko licked his lips slowly, measuring his words. "Yes." He didn't look at anyone, only at the overgrown grass beside his boot.

Exasperated, Mama stood and put a fist on her hip. "And?"

"And . . . we contended." Jouko finally turned his head just enough to look at their mother, intent on avoiding Aino's gaze.

"And?" This time it was Papa who'd grown impatient.

Jouko closed his eyes and lowered his head. "And Vane won."

"Did you lose your sleigh to him?" Papa asked. "Why didn't the man take your horse?"

Aino shot a look at her parents, begging them to stop. For whatever reason, Jouko had returned broken. Pestering him right now would accomplish nothing.

"You're home," Aino said. "That's all we wanted. He let you come home." She slipped her hands around one of his.

"I'm fine . . . now." Jouko left his right hand in hers but rubbed the other one nervously, back and forth, on his thigh. A row of tears tumbled down his cheeks like beads falling off a necklace. "He could have killed me easily. Mama, Papa, you were right; *no one* can beat Old Reliable."

The horse got antsy and pawed the ground. Papa stepped over to the horse. He stroked her neck and spoke quietly to calm her down. When Jouko didn't continue, Papa led the horse toward the barn. Mama and Sanna went back inside, but Aino remained with her brother. She sensed he felt alone and needed someone with him.

He must feel shame for failing, but he shouldn't.

"Don't cry," Aino said softly.

Jouko pulled his hand from hers and raked his fingers through his hair. "I have reason enough for crying. The old man, he—he sang a malicious magic, spells I will lament all my days. I—I'll weep forever because of what I've done."

He stood suddenly and took several paces away from her, then spun around and returned. She stood expectantly. When he reached her, he took her hands, and looked pitifully into her eyes.

Fear pricked the edges of Aino's heart. "Jouko, what did you do?"

"Something to save my life. In a moment of panic, it seemed to be my only option." He spoke rapidly now, the words spilling from him like a rapid stream with winter runoff.

"What did you do?" she repeated

With shaky fingers, Jouko untied the ribbon from his buttonhole and handed it to her. "I did it to keep my promise."

Skeptical, she took the ribbon but said not a word.

"Please forgive me." He folded her hand over the ribbon. It looked ragged and muddy.

"You're alive," Aino said matter-of-factly. "What is there to be forgiven?"

Her brother's eyes grew watery. When he spoke, he practically spat the words out. "I promised you as his wife."

A heartbeat of silence followed. Aino couldn't breathe. This wasn't her brother; this was her executioner.

The door opened, and Mama flew outside. "What good fortune!" She must have been listening at the door. Sanna stood there too, but with a more somber expression. She understood what their brother had done.

Aino lowered her eyes to the ribbon, no longer crimson but rust-colored. Her ears had heard her brother's words, but she could *not* comprehend them. Could not *believe* them.

It could not be true. It could *not*. Marry an old man, become caretaker to a duffer, a bed warmer for an ancient, wrinkled, cruel . . .

Never!

Her mother continued to gush. "What luck! No need for tears, my dear boy. This is a time for *celebration*. To have Vane as my kinsman—imagine! Of course, I always assumed Sanna would marry first, but if there was ever an acceptable exception to tradition, this is it!" She threw her arms around Aino, who stood stiff as a pine board. Her mother squeezed, hard.

Mama raised her arms to the sky in praise and spun around and around. "Remember back at the market, how I said I wanted Vane for a son-in-law? The gods must have listened, because I got my wish." Her hands crossed over her breast as she stopped spinning. "Such an honor."

When Aino didn't reply, her mother marched over. Her skirts rustled with the movement. "Daughter, come now. Thank your brother for his wonderful gift."

With a blink, Aino returned to the present. The hideous, horrible, unbelievable—present. Her entire body trembled, whether with anger or fear or disbelief, she wasn't sure. She lifted her eyes not to her mother but to Jouko. "I cannot marry Vane." She spoke in measured tones, belying the fury within her. "I *will* not."

Jouko's eyes widened in fear. "But—you must. He'll come for you soon. You cannot refuse. We made a contract. He'll take you, and if you refuse him, he'll kill both of us. We sang a pact, he and I. We are bound by magic. You are bound to him by magic. Y-you *must* marry him."

"Aino, Aino, Aino." Mama came over and patted her daughter's arm. She spoke as if Aino stood no higher than her knee. "Your brother is right; you can't refuse Old Reliable. If he wants you, he will have you. When he rides in on his sleigh one afternoon to take you, there will be naught you can do about it. That's how the magic works, my dear. You should know that. But you don't really want to refuse Vane, of course." She smiled lovingly, as if she'd just informed Aino that her favorite supper would be on the table that night.

"Marriage to him would be a living death," Aino said flatly.

Jouko gripped her arm; Aino winced. When he noticed the pain on her face, he let go. "But you *must*. Even if you never forgive me for the promise, it is already made. Please understand—I offered him everything I had, but he would have none until I offered . . . *you*."

If she became Vane's wife, she'd never again see her true love. *Paavo, oh, Paavo.* She could still feel his kiss on her lips, his hand in hers, his heartbeat as she pressed her ear to his chest. Tears formed in her eyes and spilled over.

She lifted her chin. "I was never yours to offer." Her voice even sounded like the dead. Would she ever feel alive again? Feel *happy* again?

Mama scoffed. "I've had quite enough of this nonsense. I see no cause for weeping."

"But there *is* cause." Aino turned on her. "Such cause!" She shook her head in disbelief. How could her mother not see this betrayal, this tragedy of the worst kind? Did she genuinely wish an old man for her daughter's husband?

Oh, Paavo. You are cause enough for weeping. Her heart ached as intensely for him as it raged against her brother. *How could Jouko throw me into the fire to save himself—destroy my hopes and dreams with a single promise?*

She took a bold step toward her brother. "You are a greater fool than I ever supposed. It would be better for me to swim with the fishes in the sea than to spend my days being the comfort of an old man. Let Vane *have* my brother, who was so filled with pride and folly and selfishness that he insisted on dueling the best singer the world has ever known."

With hot tears her eyes, Aino turned and fled into the woods.

Chapter Seven

Aino ran blindly through the trees, heedless of bushes slapping and scratching her skin. She jumped over fallen logs and dodged boulders, desperate to escape. She got a stitch in her side but refused to stop, as if she could undo the cursed contract if only she could create enough distance between herself and her brother.

Her shoe caught on a tree root, which pitched her forward. She landed sprawled on the forest floor. Only after she caught her breath and pushed up did she feel angry scrapes on her palms and face from rough bark, switches, and who knew what else she'd run past in desperation.

She crawled to the nearest tree with a solid trunk, unable to stand or walk. After far too much effort, she managed to turn around and sit against the tree. She pulled her knees up and wrapped her arms around them then sobbed. The salty tears made her scratches sting, but she hardly noticed; the pain in her breast hurt so much more. A horrid keening sound went through the forest, sounding like a wounded animal.

Aino tried to listen, to find the other creature who suffered as she did, only to realize that the sounds came from her own throat. She didn't want to rest; she wanted to flee, but knew that in the end, no one could escape Vane if he wanted to find them.

If only we hadn't gone to the market. Then Vane wouldn't have seen me.

No, even that wouldn't have been enough to stop it all: Vane still would have come, and Jouko would have been compared to him anyway. Jouko would have become just as upset. He would have gone to challenge the wizard regardless.

One thing would be different if I hadn't gone to the market, Aino thought. *Jouko wouldn't have been able to use me to bargain with, so he'd be dead.* No matter what she'd done that day, they were doomed to one kind of tragedy or another. If only the wretched singer had never come. His arrival—that's what created all of this mischief in the first place.

And my proud brother. Stupid, stupid boy.

Footfalls sounded on the forest floor. Pine needles crackled and twigs snapped. Aino tried to hold in her ragged breath. She swiped both hands across her cheeks to hide her tears from whoever lurked out there. Appearing weak would not improve her situation. Yet anyone who glanced at her would note her tears, which would not stop. Scratches covered her face. Her eyes were surely red and swollen. They would likely be so for the rest of her life, because every day, she would weep over what Jouko had done. She would weep every moment she had to spend with the leather-faced wizard.

The footfalls drew closer and stopped. "Aino?" a voice called. A gentle, familiar—and oh, so welcome—voice. "Is that you?"

A sliver of hope pierced the dark fog of misery. "Paavo?"

He called again, and she turned to search the direction she'd come from. There he was, not fifty paces away, but almost invisible due to the thick woods. She knew the moment he spotted her too, as he broke into a sprint. When he reached her, he sank to his knees and touched her face, but she got to her knees and threw her arms about him, clung to him as if he were life itself. "How did you find me? Did someone send you?"

"No," he said, confused. "I was on my way home from my traps and heard crying. I didn't know it was you." He pulled away and looked over her. "You're all scratched up. Why are you out here? You could have gotten lost."

Why am I out here? He doesn't know.

Paavo turned one of her arms this direction and then that, followed by the other, as if looking for injuries. "Are you seriously hurt?"

Oh, she was so much more than hurt. But he meant physical wounds.

"No," she said.

But Paavo clearly heard misery in her voice, because his attention snapped to her face. Worry blanketed his expression. "Aino, tell me. What happened?"

At first, she couldn't speak. How could she possibly tell him the horrible truth?

"Any word of your brother?"

She closed her eyes, which sent more tears down her cheeks.

"Is he . . ."

She shook her head. "He's alive. He's back."

"Truly? That's wonder—" Paavo cut himself off. His brows furrowed. "Did he return cursed or wounded, or . . ."

"Jouko is fine." She grasped Paavo's hands and clung to them. "But he's done something so, so awful."

Paavo must have sensed her desperation, because he pulled her into his embrace. "Tell me all of it."

In his arms, she nodded, and they sat together on the forest floor for several minutes as Aino soaked in strength from Paavo's embrace. He didn't insist she speak before she was ready. At last she told the tale.

"Vane nearly killed him. Jouko offered all of his possessions, but Vane refused until . . ." She shuddered. Paavo didn't press her to continue; he simply stroked her back in circles—a motion that calmed her. "Jouko made one last offer, which Vane accepted." Now that the moment had come, she couldn't speak the words. She shook her head miserably against his shirt. "I won't lose you. I *won't*."

Paavo held her tight with one hand and stroked her hair with the other. "You won't. Tell me what happened."

She forced herself to pull away, and she sat on her heels. *I must tell him.* Yet she could not bear to see his eyes when he learned of the curse, so she looked away.

"Aino, what is it?" He gently took her face in both hands and lifted it to his. "Tell me."

Her entire body shook with fear and sorrow. What if speaking about the curse would draw Vane to her sooner, or have some other consequence she couldn't imagine?

Their eyes held for several seconds, and she searched the depths of his. Perhaps, together, they could find a solution. She sighed heavily to even out her breath. It didn't work.

"Jouko . . ." She had to swallow to moisten her throat enough to speak. "Jouko promised me."

Paavo's worried expression now had a layer of confusion added to it. "I don't understand."

"He promised Vane that he could have me as his wife." Speaking the bitter truth meant she was no longer alone in her suffering. Some consolation, she supposed.

Paavo's face went ashen. Then he gathered her close to his chest once more and held her tight. "What Jouko promised does not matter. Vane cannot—*will not*—have you." He spoke with determination. His voice reassured Aino; they'd find a way out of this mess.

"Vane will not have me," Aino repeated. "I will *not* marry him." She slowly pulled back. She rested her hands on Paavo's chest. "But Vane *will* come. What will we do then? When I refuse to marry, he'll kill my brother. And because of the contract, even then, Vane could sing me away with him, and I'd be trapped."

He reached up and placed his hands over hers. "We'll find a solution, somehow."

"Yes," Aino said, wiping her cheeks with both hands. She would be brave. No one faint of heart ever overcame a curse. "Yes, we will."

"Perhaps the old man will see reason."

"I cannot see how."

"We'll search for magic equal to Vane's to save us from your brother's folly." He kissed her forehead, eyes filled with tears. "I cannot lose you. We will find a way."

She clung to the edges of his coat. If only she could know that all would be well, know that in a year, she would bake bread for Paavo, help him stretch pelts. And someday, she would bear children, and they would rear them together. "How can you be so sure?"

"We'll find a way, because we have a power he lacks." He sounded so sure.

In surprise, Aino lifted her eyes to his again. "What's that?"

"Love. No magic can create love or match its power. With love, we'll find a way."

"You're right. Of course." Aino put every ounce of faith she could into the words, yet her heart doubted. She could see no way of escape.

Paavo lifted the flap of the pouch at his belt. "I bought you a gift yesterday and have carried it with me since." He pulled his hand out to reveal a shiny silver brooch, a solki with clusters of lingonberries engraved with a light, skillful touch. Sunlight filtering through the trees glanced off the surface. He laid it onto her outstretched hand.

"It's real silver," she breathed.

This solki was slightly larger than her palm—definitely bigger than any she'd seen in town. The engravings circled a hole in the center, which would let the blue of her bridal dress show through.

"It's perfect." With one finger, Aino traced the lines of the engraved berries.

"And it's yours." Paavo took the solki and opened the clasp. He pinned the silver circle at the front of her dress. She stroked what was easily the most valuable item she'd ever owned. Then Paavo leaned down and kissed her cheek. Aino's heart fluttered.

"Now all the world will know you are taken—even the old man. When he sees this pinned to your dress, he'll know that someone put it there—and he'll think twice before taking you."

I hope you're right. A cacophony of emotions confused Aino's heart—joy and love clashed with fear for herself and for Paavo. For her foolish brother. A tear escaped each eye.

She didn't dare vocalize the thought or mention that she didn't yet dare wear the solki openly. What if the sight angered Vane? What if Mama flew into a rage and refused to allow Paavo and Aino to see each other again?

No, for now, the solki needed to remain hidden. She'd try to wear it, but it would have to remain under a scarf or pinned inside her dress.

She leaned close and kissed his lips. "My heart will always belong to you."

"And mine to you." Paavo kissed her again.

Footsteps sounded nearby, and the two flew apart and to their feet like a pair of startled seagulls. Aino whipped around toward the source, one hand over her precious solki. Paavo gripped her forearm so tightly she winced. Neither moved a muscle, both surely worried that Vane had come. To their relief, someone else materialized through the trees—a tall young man with a shock of wild blond hair.

"Jouko." Aino's heart thudded heavily in her chest. While she was glad she hadn't seen Vane, her traitorous brother wasn't welcome either. "What are you doing here?"

"Looking for you." His voice sounded flat, devoid of life. His face looked drawn, with his eyes reddened as if he'd shed rivers of tears and might shed more at any moment. Aino had never seen her brother cry, not even when, as a boy, he'd fallen off the roof and broken his arm.

Guilt clearly burdened him. For a moment, the sight melted some of Aino's bitterness. But then she remembered what he felt guilty about, and fury flamed into her breast again. Her own flesh and blood had fed her to a wolf to save his own selfish hide.

"What do you want?" she asked sharply. She glared at him, a silent threat: ask no questions about her and Paavo or why she had an expensive new solki. Keep quiet about it and do not mention it at home.

Jouko lowered his head with dejection. "No matter what anyone says, I know I have wronged you." He gestured toward the solki. "Now I see how far my crime reaches. I did not know your heart already belonged to any man."

Aino took Paavo's hand in hers. "My heart has long since been given to Paavo. As you see, we have plans to be married."

"When Vane's claim is undone," Paavo added.

"If it can be," Jouko said. He took a deep breath. "And that's exactly what I plan to do."

"How?" Aino asked eagerly.

Paavo took a step closer to Jouko. "Yes, do you know a song to reverse the contract?"

"No," Jouko said. Not the answer they'd hoped for, but at least it was the truth. "Much of what he sang was new to me—songs and techniques I've never heard." He paused, swallowed, and took a breath. "Vane is a far more accomplished singer than I." The admission clearly required much of him.

"What is your plan?" Paavo demanded. He sounded not at all sympathetic toward Jouko's plight. She loved him all the more for his loyalty.

Jouko lifted his chin slightly, as he had to force a drop of self-respect back into his spine. "At first light, I will travel to Seppo's to study."

That made sense. Aino and Paavo exchanged looks. It wasn't a clear plan, but if any library in the world had the answers, it would be the master Seppo's.

The library of Jouko's former master was a huge room filled to bursting with rare leather-bound volumes of magical songs and theories. Aino would pray that one of those books held information Jouko could find and use. He couldn't have studied them all in his six-year apprenticeship. On the other hand, Seppo's library might contain a useful tidbit Jouko had learned years before but had simply forgotten or had passed over.

"Can Seppo help, then?" Aino asked. "I've heard rumors that he's sick."

"Unfortunately, you've heard correctly," Jouko said. "When I visited over the winter solstice, he was quite ill. He'd gone almost blind and totally senile. He didn't recognize me— or his wife. I'll have to search through his books myself."

Hard to believe that the powerful Seppo could have become so frail. As a singer and blacksmith, he'd created some of the most magical items in history, including the legendary sampo, which lay broken at the bottom of the sea, still churning salt.

Seppo no longer forged new magical creations. He no longer trained apprentices. Instead, he spent his days in bed, broken, churning out broken songs in delirium. At least, those were the rumors. Jouko was probably the last person from Marjala to have seen him.

He ran a hand through his hair, leaving it disheveled. "I'm to inherit Seppo's books when he dies, and Eva knows that. She'll let me in." His eyes narrowed with determination, and he turned to face Aino directly. "Sweet sister, I vow to spend every day in search of a way to fix this great evil I have done to you. If I exhaust Seppo's library, I will seek out other singers for their knowledge. I will search for a way to free you

73

for the rest of my life. It should have been my life lost, not yours. I will give mine up if that's the price of setting you free."

"Thank you, Jouko." Aino's heart softened toward her brother. Her heart swelled. Between the three of them, surely a solution would be found.

Her brother cleared his throat and shifted his feet. "I'll—I'll go now." A hand went up to cover his face. He sniffed and turned away.

"Wait." Aino reached forward and touched his arm.

He paused in his step, head still lowered.

"I believe in you, Jouko, remember?"

Slowly, he turned to her, his expression pained and hopeful at once.

"I always have," Aino continued. She put her arms around his waist and hugged him. "And I forgive you."

He closed his eyes and wrapped his arms about her, hard. A sob escaped his throat, and he cried, "How I wish I could forgive myself!"

Chapter Eight

The sun had scarcely crested the horizon the next morning when Jouko awoke and dressed, eager to be on his way to Seppo's. He made a breakfast of a thick rye cracker slathered with butter and a tin mug of piimä. Before his departure, he quietly opened his sisters' bedroom door and peered in.

Aino slept peacefully at the edge of the shared bed, her red hair spread across her pillow. Somehow, she looked much as she had as a young girl, when they were children, teasing each other while swimming in the lake. Someone kind and good like his younger sister didn't deserve to have her life thrown away.

As, unfortunately, he had doomed her to.

"I'll find a way," he whispered. "I promise."

Aino stirred and rolled to her side. Jouko carefully closed the door. On his way out of the house, he put on his cap and jacket.

In the barn, he saddled his fastest horse, eager to reach Seppo's early to make the most of every minute in the library. As Jouko led the horse outside, he passed the spot where his sleigh used to be kept. He paused in his step, noting the silhouette where dust had fallen around the sleigh. A physical ache twisted in his chest. He'd been so proud of that sleigh. He'd bought it with money he'd earned himself with his work. The sleigh had served him well. Yet he'd left it behind in the wood because he would never sing again. Not unless—not *until*—he could sing to free his sister.

He shook his head to chase away the sadness, then clicked his tongue to urge the horse along. Good thing he didn't need to carry supplies in a sleigh, he supposed. Seppo didn't live far, and if all went well, Jouko might be home in time for a hot supper with his family. If the gods favored him, he'd return bearing good news.

Outside, he adjusted the saddle. He supposed that one benefit to riding was that he wouldn't have to stay to well-worn roads, as would with a sleigh. On horseback, he could gallop through forests no matter how thick.

He was about to mount the horse when the front door of the house opened. A flash of his mother's yellow scarf made him turn around. He thought he'd left without anyone waking. Hopefully she'd come outside to milk the cows.

Alas, Mama did not appear surprised to see him—rather the opposite. She planted a fist on one hip. "Where do you think you're going?" she demanded, both eyebrows raised in challenge.

"To visit Seppo. He's not well, as I'm sure you know. It's been too long since I saw him last." Jouko shot her his most charming smile—the one that had always softened her in the past, the one he used as a boy at the spring equinox celebration. With that smile, he'd always managed to get another bowl of mämmi, an annual treat made of malted rye, with extra honey and cream. He stroked his horse's neck and hoped he sounded relaxed. "No need to worry. I should be back by supper." He moved to mount the horse, but Mama marched over and grabbed the reins.

"I suspected as much," she said. "And I forbid it." She pressed her lips together so hard that they nearly disappeared into her face.

Normally, Jouko couldn't bear to go against his mother's wishes, but as much as he wished he could stay, he simply couldn't. Over her shoulder, he saw the spot where he'd told Aino what he'd done. He could still see the horror in her eyes.

"I'm sorry, but I must go. For Aino's sake." He hadn't said a word about hoping to learn how to break the curse. Clearly, he hadn't needed to.

"Unsaddle your horse this minute." She pointed to the stable, arm fully extended.

"Try to understand," Jouko pled. "I must fix this."

She scoffed. "There is nothing to be fixed, and *everything* to be lost." Her eyes narrowed, creating a deep wrinkle between them. "You will put in jeopardy the future of our family.

If—no, *when*—Aino marries Vane, we will live like royalty! Don't you see?" Mama continued to plead. "Can you imagine never again having to scrape by? Look at the calluses on my hands. Look! After they marry, I will never again have to work my fingers raw to be sure we can eat. We will have no more empty stomachs through the long, dark winters. Vane will be kinsman, and he will provide for us."

Jouko wished he could give in. He understood why Mama wanted this. Clear memories of empty flour barrels and bellies aching from hunger were almost enough to sway him. But not quite. "Goodbye, Mama."

"Think of yourself," she said, her words coming out faster now. "You could learn from Vane, become as powerful as he is. Think how you'll be revered. Never again will you have to plug a leaky boat. Oh, no. You'll use your magic for far greater deeds. You will be remembered with glorious stories!"

The temptation grabbed hold of Jouko; he could picture everything his mother described. But no. He wouldn't allow his pride to rule him again. "This isn't about you, and it isn't about me. This is about Aino."

"Selfish boy! Selfish girl!" Mama's grip tightened on the reins; her knuckles turned white. But then her face softened. She pressed a hand to his heart. "My sweet boy." She almost sounded as if she spoke to a babe. "Don't you want what is best for your *family*?"

He gently but firmly removed her hand and took the reins from her grasp. "I want what is best for *Aino*—and that certainly isn't life with an old man she despises, no matter how powerful his magic." He mounted his horse, which forced her to stepped aside. "Goodbye, Mama."

He kicked his heels, and the horse shot off. Behind him, his mother wailed, but he paid her no mind. Today his actions had to be for someone besides himself—for his beloved sister who didn't deserve to be married against her will to anyone, let alone to the man who'd humiliated Jouko to the dust.

Or, rather, to the swamp.

He gritted his teeth and pushed his horse far harder than necessary, practically flying through the trees. In less than half an hour, he reached Seppo's homestead. Jouko reined in and eyed the windows, which were yet shuttered for the night.

He spied no signs of life inside. Perhaps he'd come much too early in the day. Seppo and Eva were likely still asleep.

He dismounted and led the horse past Seppo's forge. It stood cold and still now, the windows draped in cobwebs. With a sigh, Jouko continued to the barn, which he knew almost as well as the forge, for in addition to his magical studies, Jouko had mucked stalls, collected eggs, and shoed horses.

He had memories from the first year of his apprenticeship, when he'd sat on a barrel in the barn, trying to copy Seppo's voice and intonation in his earliest studies with the most basic tunes. What a thrill it had been the first time he'd made a shovel dance in the air. Jouko had worked for nearly a week to master that one, but by the end, he had the shovel twirling and hopping about better than many of his friends could dance themselves.

Seppo and Eva wouldn't mind housing a horse for the day—or several days in a row. He'd gone senile and probably wouldn't even recognize his former apprentice. But Eva would, and Jouko hoped she'd welcome him rather than ask why he hadn't visited since winter.

In one of the small stalls, he removed the bridle, saddle, and blanket then brushed the horse down. He found a barrel of oats by the door, surely there for Seppo and Eva's horse, which stood in the only other stall. Jouko scooped a ladleful into a bucket for his horse.

When he left the stable, he noted the shutters about the kitchen window glowing with a golden light. Good. Eva, at least, was up now. She'd always been kind to Jouko, like another—gentler—mother. He went to the door and rapped lightly as to not cause her to start. After shuffling footsteps, the latch slid open, and then the door swung wide.

"Jouko, my dear boy. What a surprise!" Eva stepped out to him and reached up to place both hands on his cheeks. When he was younger—and shorter—she'd done the same, always kissing his forehead. Now that he was more than a head taller, he leaned down and kissed her forehead.

"I hope you don't mind my coming so early. I need your help."

"Not at all. Come, come, I'm making some pine needle for Seppo's cough, but I'll make a bit more for the two of us. I seem to remember that you liked it back in the day."

Jouko nodded. He remembered. The tea was tolerable, but he'd never liked it. Seppo, however always insisted that was good for keeping one's eyes strong for long hours of study. "That would be wonderful." The taste would certainly bring back a flood of memories.

"Good, good. You can tell me all about your worries."

Jouko went inside and closed the door behind him. "I have come across a need for a particular type of spell," he said. "Could I study in the library?"

"Of course. That makes the tea an even better idea, doesn't it?" Eva chuckled. She retrieved a copper kettle from the fireplace and poured a cupful of hot water for him. "The books are yours already in all but name. But first, sit down and have some tea." She added fresh pine needles to a pretty tea infuser and placed it into the cup to steep the tea. Seppo had surely made the infuser himself.

Jouko wondered if the master wizard had added any-thing magical to it, or if the infuser simply held herbs for tea. Eva had always loved her tea, and would drink it all day—let it steep for hours—if she had her wish. As much as he would enjoy a cup of tea, especially made from something other than pine needs, he wasn't here for a social call. He eyed the library door, just visible from the kitchen. Behind that door lay a room packed with bookshelves. And one of those books held the answer to saving Aino.

His hostess's gaze followed his. "Eager, are we?" She chuckled. "Forget tea for now. It'll be here when you're ready for it. Go. Study and read to your heart's content."

"Thank you." Jouko stood there with his cap in his hands. "You have no idea how deeply important this is to me."

She led him across the house to the library door. She took a key from around her neck and slipped it into the famil-iar iron padlock. "Spend as much time in there as you need." She removed the lock and opened the door.

Dust-filled, musty air whooshed out, and with it came a wave of memories. Jouko could almost see Seppo in the chair in the corner, with his pipe, saying, "Again. Only this time, enunciate the last two syllables. And you were flat on the first phrase."

Eva stepped to the side, but Jouko didn't go in right away. He hadn't counted on how odd it would seem to cross that threshold without his teacher's permission. "How is Seppo?" he asked, gazing at the chair in the corner.

"About the same as last time," Eva said. He turned to her, unsure if that was good or bad news. She gave him a weak smile. "Some days he doesn't know me. On others, he sings songs he's forgotten—or makes some up—and I have a mess to clean up afterward. The other day, he broke his supper dishes." She laughed at that, though a thread of melancholy wound through it. "Now go, go." She shooed him toward the library. "Find what it is you're looking for, and let me know when you're hungry. I'll fix up some of your favorite reindeer stew for later."

"Thank you, Eva." Jouko stepped inside and breathed in the familiar scent. He felt transported back in time, as if he had lessons to recite and vocal exercises to perform. The room felt smaller. How many years had passed since he'd been in here? He looked around. Where to begin? As he walked along the walls, he recalled how the library was organized.

One shelf had books of songs recorded by Sauli, an ancient singer of the North.

Books by Taneli, a more recent wizard known for his power over weather, lined another shelf. Jouko remembered the precious volumes and looking over the songs—how to made rain, conjure wind, and control rivers. Those were never his specialty.

More and more dusty books stared out at Jouko, mocking him. What if he ignored the very book that held the key to defeating Vane? The room held too many possibilities for failure.

Eventually he selected two books to begin with. The first was penned by Otso, who'd penned a volume about the history of magical song. Jouko hoped to find clues in it about the nature of Vane's tricks. The second volume, thinner than the other, was one Jouko had abandoned in his final year. At the time, Seppo encouraged him to focus on his specific strengths and interests—and Jouko never imagined that he'd care about Hannu's theories on reversing spells.

Today, Jouko's hopes lay largely in that one small book. He knew a little about undoing spells beyond the method Vane had used to free him—singing the charm in reverse. But even if Jouko could have remembered the contract well enough for that, he couldn't reverse the magic. Only the person who first sang the spell could. He prayed to the gods that he would find a way to reverse other wizards' spells or how to release someone from a contract. Either would do.

For the rest of the day, Jouko pored over pages. Book after book, he scribbled notes with a sharpened length of charcoal onto sheets of vellum. When Eva poked her nose in at midday, he said he wasn't hungry. When the sun sank past the horizon, she quietly slipped in with a small lamp and left it beside him.

By that point, Jouko had amassed six stacks of books on the desk—but no answers. Knowing it would be time to go home soon, he looked over the day's notes. Simple incantations. Reversals to fix errors in songs. Calling a bear for favors. *As if a bear could stop Vane.*

Jouko shook his head at his own foolish hope about that one and crossed off that idea with the charcoal, which he'd worn to a nub. He read notes twice more, only to realize that none of it was of the slightest bit of use. He crumpled it all up, marched to the kitchen, and opened the front of the stove. He'd spent an entire day here, and for what? He glared at his handwriting, which mocked him.

He wanted to shove it all into the fire but hesitated. The notes might have been useless, but the vellum itself was valuable. And he'd been about to impulsively burn it? Seppo would be ashamed of him for wasting a single sheet of it. Then again, he'd already wasted plenty. The sheets were good for little now but starting fires.

Eva quickly draped a pair of newly dipped candles over a drying rack then hurried over to him. "You don't want to do that." She grabbed his arm and eased the sheets of vellum out of his grip. She placed the stack on the table and used a poker to close the stove door.

The clink of the metal brought Jouko back to his senses. She was right, of course. His chin sank to his chest.

She led him to the table, where she eased him into a chair. "No solution yet?" Eva dished up a steaming bowl of reindeer stew. Despite his frustration, Jouko's mouth watered. He hadn't eaten since the cracker and butter at dawn.

"No answers yet," he said, taking the bowl. "This smells delicious. Thank you."

Eva dished herself some stew and sat beside him. "May I ask what it is you're in search of? Perhaps I can help."

He took one bite and another, then unloaded his worries, telling Eva of his childish challenge and all that had happened since.

"By the heavens," Eva said, one hand splayed across her chest. "I'm amazed you're alive to tell the tale."

"I shouldn't be alive," Jouko said. "It was a half-witted thing to do; I know that now." He drew a hand down his chin and crossed his arms with a sigh. "I must fix the trouble I've put my sister in."

Eva put a hand on his arm. "If there's anyone who can fix it, that person is you."

He nodded toward the stairs. "Or Seppo."

She didn't look where he'd indicated. "A *younger* Seppo," she corrected softly, but nodded in agreement. A few years ago, her husband might have been a great help in such a matter.

After scooping the last of the stew, Jouko sighed, stood, and put on his hat. "Thank you for supper. I'll be back tomorrow, if I may."

"You are welcome to spend as much time in the library as you need."

"Thank you." He stepped toward the door, but Eva called him back.

"In fact, don't go. Stay the night. Take the guest room at the top of the stairs and get a fresh start on your search as soon as you wake."

He smiled, a pebble of warmth in his chest. Hope, perhaps. "Thank you."

In truth, he didn't want to go home yet. His mother would be waiting up for him. She'd demand to know what he'd found. And in the morning, she'd try harder to stop him from.

He glanced toward the stairs. "Could I—could I see Seppo tonight? Perhaps that would spark his memory and—"

"No." The word was clipped. Eva pressed her lips together and shook her head. "He wouldn't like that. And it would be no good. Today he's been in, well, no condition for visitors." She handed over a slice of rye bread, muttered an apology, and scurried back to her candle making.

"I understand," he said. "Thank you again for supper."

Jouko spent the night in a small room with a short bed. He wouldn't have to face Mama tonight, but she wasn't the only reason he dreaded home. How he could go home, see Aino, and tell her he'd failed?

Tomorrow I must find an answer. He stared at the ceiling. *I must.* So fatigued was he from the day's work, that he fell asleep almost the moment the thought entered his mind.

When he entered Eva's kitchen for breakfast, she greeted him with a warm smile. "I have bread fresh from the oven if you'd like some." The dark rounds were cooling on the wooden table.

"I would, thank you."

Eva cut two large slices and added butter and a hunk of goat cheese. As he ate, she sat beside him and said pensively, "After you went to bed last night, I wondered whether Seppo could still help, even with how testy he'd been." She lifted a hand as if ready to argue. "On such days, he'll only speak to me, so there wouldn't have been a point in sending you up, I assure you."

Jouko hardly dared hope. He swallowed a bite of bread quickly, and it scraped its way down. "Did you speak to him, then?"

"I did. Sometimes, just *sometimes*, talk of magic will wake part of his mind."

"What did he say?"

"Only that he was certain someone had stolen the sampo, but that's not unusual." Eva rolled the edge of her apron. "I'll try again today, if you like."

"Do you think—may—could *I* speak to him today?" Jouko knew what the answer would likely be but hoped anyway. "Perhaps, as his last apprentice, I could spark a memory."

A sharp shake of her head put that question to rest. "I know it's hard to understand, but he wouldn't want you, of all people, to see him like this. I don't think it would do much good anyway. His good days are farther and farther apart." Her eyes were wistful, as if thinking about decades past. She sighed then clapped a hand on the table as if that would banish the dreary mood. "But when I awoke, I *did* think of something that might help. I know where Seppo keeps his most important texts, the ones with the rarest and most powerful spells."

"On the shelf beside his chair."

"No, not those," Eva said. "I mean songs he has never taught to any apprentice, not even you. Such texts are traditionally not passed on until the death of a master." She bit her lip and tilted her head to one side. "I think perhaps this is an extenuating circumstance."

Seppo had secret spells? He'd hidden them well, had never given a hint that they existed. Jouko felt ready to jump out of his skin, eager to get started with the secret books. Had they been passed to Seppo by *his* master?

Eva held up a hand again, clearly trying to quell any false hopes. "Now there may be nothing in them, but I'll let you read them in case there's a chance."

"Show me." Jouko tossed the last bit of bread into his mouth and stood.

Once again, he followed Eva to the library. She went in first, and headed straight for the little round table on the other side of Seppo's chair. The little table had always been draped in off-white linen. Jouko remembered the table all too well. He had plenty of memories of the four different ashtrays Seppo always kept on it. He could always tell what mood Seppo was in because of which pipe he used—the copper when he was happy and optimistic, the silver for a foul mood, the engraved bronze one with the when agitated, and the pewter pipe with the oval bowl when fatigued. As an apprentice, Jouko always hoped to see the copper.

Eva knelt before the table and lifted the linen drape. She pulled out a small trunk secured with a golden lock. To think it had been under there, so near, yet hidden all these years. Eva carried it to the desk at the center of the room, then used another key from the chain around her neck to open it. The box held four books, each with cracking leather covers and fragile vellum pages. They looked veritably ancient even compared to the decades-old books on the library shelves. Jouko worried they'd turn to dust if he touched them.

"These will be yours soon," Eva said. "Since Seppo isn't gone, I suppose I shouldn't be sharing them with you *quite* yet." Her tone implied that the day wasn't too far off.

"Thank you." Jouko's heart pounded, and his fingers itched to open the volumes.

Eva silently left him alone and closed the library door behind her. Gingerly, Jouko drew out the first book and set the fragile volume on the table. He sat down and reverently opened the book. The leather cover groaned with its first movement in years.

The author listed on the front page was Rauno.

Jouko's brow furrow. He knew of no singer by that name. The title only confused him more: *Songs of the Immortals*.

He knew of immortal creatures, of course. Every child learned of them from nursery rhymes. But no one had ever seen a sea maiden, a gnome, the Sun or Moon Maids, or a dozen other immortal creatures. Or at least, Jouko didn't think so. He'd always believed they were real, or had been—but that they'd died long ago.

How long ago had Rauno written of the immortals? And did they exist still? If so, what kind of magic did their songs weave? How did it vary from human magic?

Most importantly, would knowing about immortals and their songs help Aino?

Jouko turned the page and began to read.

Chapter Nine

Mama entered the house with a basket full of clean linens under her arm. She looked over the room at Sanna and Aino, grunted, and shoved the door shut with her elbow. "Aino, could you possibly *not* wear such a tragic face all the time?" She smacked the basket onto the table and threw a look at Aino, who sat in the corner by the window, hemming a new summer skirt. "You look as if you've been doomed rather than given a promise of the greatest future a girl could hope for."

Aino looked up from her needle. The solki, hidden with a scarf, suddenly felt heavy. Eventually her mother would see the brooch, but Aino would postpone that moment for as long as she could. Let Mama yell and throw every dish in the house. Aino would *not* remove Paavo's gift.

"I have every reason to feel tragic and unwell," she said evenly, drawing the needle once more. "I am sorry if I do not celebrate the fact that I'm bound to a man old enough to be *your* grandfather."

"Hush, child!" Mama said. "Don't you speak of him with such disrespectful words!"

Trying to make her mother understand was hopeless, so Aino didn't answer. She returned to her mending, but her mind refused to stray from her worries.

Jouko had been gone almost two full days, which could only mean that he hadn't learned of a way to break the contract. His continued absence kept their mother in a testy mood. For her part, Aino found her mind turning into prayers as she begged the gods to help him find a solution.

Mama's annoyance at her son's absence and her younger daughter's refusal to be happy over the impending union showed in every word and movement. She shook out the sheets one at a time as she folded them, as if angry at the poor linen. She stacked them roughly on the table.

"He'd better *not* find a way to best Vane," she said stiffly as she drew one of Papa's shirts from the basket. She snapped it in the air with far more force than necessary, all the while eyeing Aino instead of the laundry. "You and your brother are trying to reverse the best fortune this family has ever known. Jouko *will* fail to defeat Vane in this—just as he failed in their contention. You might as well put on smiles and enjoy the fact that you'll be married to a wealthy, powerful man, never again to suffer from cold or hunger."

Aino gritted her teeth and pulled so hard at the needle that the thread broke. Her mother's actions and snide remarks over the last two days had Aino felt stretched taut, like the clothesline outside pulled too tight. If Jouko didn't return soon, she'd break. Sudden noises startled her, shooting equal parts terror and hope through her veins—terror of Vane's arrival, hope of Jouko's return with a charm to save her. She practically lived by the window so she could watch the road all day. There she sewed and mended, even Sanna's share, to have more of an excuse to stay at her post and keep watch.

With disdain, Mama threw a dishcloth back into the basket and turned to face Aino, who'd begun to dread the sight of her mother's bony fist on her hip. "I've had enough of your moping. Put down that skirt and do something else for a change."

"Like . . . what?" Aino asked, both confused and defensive. She didn't consider her constant glances at the road to be *moping*. "But Sanna's skirt needs to be finished." She held up the garment as evidence.

"We're having sauna tonight," Mama said as if she hadn't heard. "The birch trees are finally leafy enough to cut from. We've gone too long without any vihtas in the sauna. Today, *you* will make the birch cuttings for the family, and you will not return until you have enough to make every one of us a good *vihta*. That is, unless you'd like to spend the night with the goats." She smiled then, but it looked more like an angry grimace.

"Leave the house?" Aino said, hating that her voice sounded uneven and revealed her fear.

Going outside would put her in danger, away from the protection the house provided. Magic wouldn't allow even Vane to steal her away while under the family's roof. The protection didn't extend beyond the roof, however, so Vane could show up and whisk her away on the family's own land. Never before had Aino considered being grateful that spells couldn't penetrate the rafters, but suddenly she understood why the term *home* was often paired with *holy.*

"Yes, leave the house," Mama scoffed. "Did you expect to find birch trees growing from the fireplace?"

"Don't make me go," Aino said. "I'd rather sleep with the goats than venture into the open."

Mama strode across the room and snatched the skirt from Aino's hands. The needle caught her palm and scraped a thin line of red. At the sudden pain, Aino sucked air between her teeth, not about to give her mother the satisfaction of tears. "Go!" She pointed at the door. Her forehead had rows of angry wrinkles. "You *will* cut enough for the whole family, and you will do it now."

Aino pressed a scrap of material against her bleeding palm. "But what about . . ." Her voice trailed off. They both knew what—or, rather, *whom* she referred to.

"What *about* my son-in-law to be?" Mama grinned crookedly. "He won't come for you tonight; don't worry your little bridal head over that. A man of his stature would claim his wife in daylight hours, and the sun has already set. The earliest he'd come is tomorrow morn."

What if he comes then? Aino's hand covered a nauseated stomach. She'd get no sleep tonight. On the other hand, she reasoned, her mother was probably right. Vane would want to be seen in daylight to be sure all knew of his arrival. Dusk wouldn't pose the same risk.

Looking through the window at the last pink streaks on the horizon, she searched the road again for Jouko and wondered what he was did right then. Would he come home yet tonight? Had he found *anything* useful in his two days of at Seppo's library?

"Daughter!" Her voice returned with a cautionary bite.

Aino reluctantly rose to her feet.

"Go." Mama jerked her head toward the door. "And make it fast."

The last admonition was unnecessary; Aino wouldn't tarry in the open a moment longer than absolutely necessary. *Vane could arrive tomorrow morn already,* she thought as she crossed to the mantel to retrieve her knife in its leather case. *Jouko, you must find an answer. Find it fast.* She slipped the knife onto her leather belt.

"I won't be long." Aino headed for the door, feeling her mother's glare on her back the entire time. *I may not be safe under the roof, but at least one good thing will come from this. I'll be away from Mama. I will never understand my mother.*

Aino went outside and headed across the grass. How could Mama *not* understand why Aino did not want to wed Vane? Even if she hadn't fallen in love with someone else, she still wouldn't want to marry a man like Vane. Did Mama *want* her younger daughter to be miserable? Surely she could see that even Jouko was miserable because of the contract.

Aino scurried behind the barn, through a small alder grove, and to the stand of birch trees nearest to the house. She kept her eye on the road, her ears alert for anyone singing. At first, she listened for her brother's voice, only to remember that if Jouko did return, he wouldn't do so while singing on sleigh.

Knife in hand, Aino reached up and cut off twigs and thin, bendable branches suitable for the bundles used to gently beat and invigorate the skin while in the sauna. She enjoyed the smell of the hot birch bundles each spring; the scent relaxed and energized all at once. Perhaps tonight she'd find a reprieve from her worries in the sauna with her mother and sister. As the oldest traditional building, the sauna was just as protected as the house—possibly even more protected, by the sauna elves. The sauna was the first structure any family built on their land, one that served as a house, bathing area, and even a clean place for mothers to give birth. Holy indeed. Yes, tonight she would feel quite safe in the sauna.

Soon she'd cut enough for her parents' bundles. She moved to another tree to cut more switches for the siblings' vihta bundles. For her, of course, but also for Sanna and Jouko.

Hopefully he would be home to use his when it was the men's turn in the sauna.

She reached up to another spot on the tree and held her knife to the base of the switch, but a sudden image appeared in her mind. One day she might cut switches and tie them together to make vihtas for her aged wizard husband. Though her hands trembled, she forced herself to keep cutting. The sooner she finished, the sooner she could go back in the house. But haste combined with shaky hands meant that she nearly cut herself with the knife again and again.

If I must make a vihta for him, I'll cut it from pine instead of soft silver birch. Let Vane slap himself with *that*—he'd deserve the scratches. For the first time since seeing Paavo yesterday, she smiled.

But then a sound froze her in place. Not just her hands but her entire body. A deep sound floated across the distance, one so deep that it seemed to resonate up from the soil beneath her feet. Music. A man's voice. Her eyes darted to the road. The tone was nothing like Jouko's; it was deep, rough.

And the song ceased as suddenly as it began. Holding her breath, Aino leaned to one side to peer through the trees but saw only a jackrabbit hopping along the packed dirt road.

Vihtas or no, she wouldn't stay outdoors a moment longer. She sheathed the knife, hurriedly gathered the armload of twigs, and headed for the house. She'd taken not five steps into the alder grove before a deep, gravelly voice sang a single word, holding out the first syllable.

"Aiiiii . . . noooooo." It came from directly behind her.

She choked on a breath, dropped the cuttings. She whirled around. "V—Vane!" Her hands flew to her chest, to her solki, still beneath her scarf. She imagined Paavo beside her.

We have love, she reminded herself. *Vane doesn't.*

"I see you were expecting me." Vane stood there, thick arms folded, a wide grin as he stepped into the open. His teeth were yellow and crooked.

Her heart pounded like a bird's wings inside her chest. Aino looked around wildly. *How* had he gotten here? Not by the road; that was certain. She took a step backward, stumbling as she ran into the pile of cuttings. The house wasn't far, but it might as well have been across an ocean. The barn was closer, but barns weren't holy. They didn't provide safety from enchantments that a home did. She caught her balance and looked around, desperate for escape.

The only person who could have possibly helped was Jouko. But she was alone.

"My, you look beautiful today." An eager smile curved his chapped lips, which were just visible through his bristly beard. "You're even prettier than when we first met. Have you made your hat yet?"

Aino swallowed a lump in her throat. "I'll never make anything from that carcass you bought me."

Vane's eyes crinkled at the edges as if he found the entire exchange amusing. "But you remember that day, don't you?" He placed a gnarled hand on a branch just as knotted and rough as his fingers. He pushed it out of his way and took a step closer. She eyed the distance between them, her breath shaky.

"Ah, you do remember," Vane said with a tap to his forehead. "I can tell."

Run! Her mind shouted the command, but her feet refused to move, as if they were trapped in tar.

"If you know that I remember that day at the market, then why don't you know that I despise you?" The words fell out of her mouth like water racing down a hill. The moment they sounded in her ears, she gasped. Surely Vane would cut her down with a single note. Her throat felt dry as straw. She clutched the sides of her skirts and managed a small step back with feet that felt leaden.

"It pleases me," he said easily, "to know that from now on, your beauty will be for no other man. You'll wear pretty things for my eyes . . . such as that solki you have on." He nodded at her scarf.

He inhaled and sang a deceptively innocent tune. The rust-orange scarf untied itself and fluttered to the ground. The solki lay exposed. As the enchantment trailed off, Aino's hand flew to the brooch.

"Exquisite," Vane said. "I've never seen the like. It pleases me that from this day forth, you will wear it for me and no other."

It is for Paavo—from Paavo.

She would rather destroy the solki than allow Vane to lay claim to it. She shook her head. "No."

"Oh, but *yes,* my dear girl," Vane said eerily. The molasses sweetness of his voice dripped with an eerie darkness. "You will wear it for me. And you will put your hair up in perfect braids with silken ribbons. You will wear *my* scarf, *my* rings and another solki. Mine. I will pay your parents well for the honor of making you my bride. That is what I came for tonight. And no, your mother didn't know I was coming."

Could he read her mind? Or did he simply deduce the truth? How many young women had he lured into his clutches over the centuries?

He chuckled and tugged his beard. "I already have the right, naturally, but I felt it only proper to honor tradition. When you're adorned with the gown and jewels I can provide, you will be as pretty as the sun in the sky."

"I don't want your gifts," Aino said. She felt lightheaded and weak, unable to fill her lungs with air.

Keep Mama inside, she prayed. If she came out and took the old man's bride money, his claim on her would be even stronger. *Bring Jouko home. I need him.*

"Think of the life you'll have with me." He took one more step closer.

"What could you provide that could possibly tempt me?" Anger made her spit the words.

Vane laughed. "Oh, I know how your family must live. I've seen it a hundred times if I have once. My first two wives were both more than grateful for what I provided for them and their families. Just think, my girl—with me, you'll never want for food. You'll have *wheat* bread to eat, not just the poor rye your family subsists on. You will have the best everything, an easy life. Imagine the only chores you do for the rest of your life are to serve me. You will be the envy of all women. Come to me, Aino. Now."

His open mouth rounded, and his chest expanded. With horror, Aino realized what he was about to do. Four notes sounded—three short, one long. As he held the final note, the solki lifted from her dress, the pin straining against the fabric.

Instead of breaking the material, the force drew her toward Vane one step at a time, as if she were a dog on a leash. "No!" She reached up and grabbed the brooch to stop the magic, only to tear a ragged hole in her dress. The clasp broke, and small pieces of metal flew in all directions, landing scattered on the forest floor like spilled lingonberries. The solki landed on a bed of leaves halfway between her and Vane.

Her wild action had cut off the spell. Once again, Aino could move easily. Yet the sweet relief of freedom was quickly tempered with bitterness that her solki would never be whole again. The reminder of her broken betrothal gift nearly made her weep.

Hateful man. But better for Paavo's gift to be broken than for Vane to use it against me with his magic.

The weathered man looked taken aback. "No?" His brow quirked in confusion, as if he couldn't understand why she wasn't eager to go to him, to live with him as man and wife. "I've outlived all of my wives, and each was happy to call me husband."

"I will never be your wife." Aino's entire body began to shake, first with anger, then with anxiety and terror. "Not for you or any singer will I tie my hair in silken ribbons or wear another solki. I'd rather have no ribbons, dresses no better than tattered potato sacks, and a face like *yours,* than marry you. I'm happy with my poor family, with only rye bread and simple clothes."

Her strength clearly took Vane off guard; he seemed unsure what to do next. She'd found an unexpected weakness in him. Taking him by surprise might be the only weapon she had against him.

"You want ribbons? You can have them!" She yanked them from her hair and threw them at his chest. "Take my trinkets—anything with the slightest beauty or value." She clawed at her shiny tin rings and even at her elaborate metal belt. She ripped the belt from its home, and it broke into several pieces. She threw whatever was left of it at his feet. Vane flinched as each item struck.

Before he could gain his bearings—or begin another song—Aino turned on her heel, her jewelry abandoned. She had one thought: *Run!* And she did so as fast as her feet could fly through the trees.

She stumbled over some rocks but kept going. At any moment, he might follow or sing her back. Her feet practically leapt up the porch steps. She tore the door open, and once inside, she slammed it shut and collapsed to the floor. She leaned against the wall and panted heavily. She was safe in the sanctity of home. For one more day, at least. The only thing that saved her this time was that Vane hadn't expected a hostile reaction. Next time, he'd be better prepared.

Unless had he *let* her go, with the knowledge that he could easily return to take her another day? He certainly had the power. Was he toying with her like a mouse, then?

She shakily stood and peered out the window. There on the road, silhouetted black against the last rosy rays of the sun, stood Vane. Her heart jolted in her chest. She pulled away and pressed her eyes closed.

"What is the matter, girl?" Mama demanded. She threw down a dish rag and strode across the room angrily.

The deep sounds of Vane's song boomed through the walls. His powerful voice got stronger. He sent a heavy wind that shook the timbers. Birch shingles broke and blew off the roof, which sent pieces of bark tumbling through the air like leaves. Mama's eyes grew large, and she braced herself against the table. Outside, the gust carried all manner of debris, throwing branches and flowers alike about like a child's game.

The melody Vane sang permeated the walls and made Aino's very bones quake.

"What is this magic?" Mama stumbled to the side and landed clumsily on a chair.

Aino braced her back against the wall. She couldn't decipher the words of the enchantment, but the oppressive tune was enough to know that Vane was *not* pleased. She cringed as wallboards dug into her shoulder blades. Her hands pressed against her ears to keep out the sound. After what felt like a lifetime, the threatening song faded to silence. Aino's breaths came in short gulps.

But it wasn't over. The old man's song began again, this time with a simple melody. Anxiety clutched at Aino's middle.

I'll be back, my dear girl.
Return will I in two days' time.
And then, dear Aino, you will be mi . . . ine.

The last word carried for several seconds.

Holding her ears with both hands, Aino slid to the floor and sobbed. Two days, he said. Now she knew exactly when to expect him. There was not a thing she could do to stop him.

"That *was* him, wasn't it?" Her mother sounded excited. Hadn't she been terrified by the storm he'd caused only moments before?

With a disappointed shake of her head, Mama strode back to the table to finish with the cream, which had sloshed out of the bucket during the storm. At the table, she paused and looked around the room. "Wait. Where are the birch bundles?"

When Aino didn't answer right way, Mama came over to her on the floor, where she was still sat in a curled-up ball. "What's the matter with you?"

I'm losing my life. But aloud she answered the first question. "I dropped the bundles when I fled Vane."

Her mother opened her mouth to protest, but Aino would have none of it. She shook her head to silence any protest. Tears streaked down her cheeks. She rose to her knees and cried, "I have enough cause for complaining. I've now lost all my jewelry. I've lost my ribbons. Even my belt is gone, destroyed. Is *that* reason enough for weeping?"

She crossed to a chair, where she dropped, spent. What could she do now? Two days before he returned. Even if she stayed inside then, Vane would find a way around the protection of the roof. She couldn't stay inside forever. He'd wait, find a way.

But he probably wouldn't need to wait at all; given the opportunity, her mother would simply open the door, and invite him inside. With an invitation, he could cross the threshold. And then Mama would hand over her youngest living child.

"Do not weep, sweet daughter."

Aino looked up, surprised at the sudden gentle tone. Their eyes met, and Mama went on.

"I have a surprise that will dry your eyes. I'll show you in the morning."

"Very well." Aino couldn't utter a word of thanks for the unknown gift. She hoped that the surprise—whatever it might be—would be something to dry her tears. But it would likely be a new belt and some rings to replace the ones she'd lost. Trinkets wouldn't make her happy.

If only I could have my solki back.

She had two days. No more. But then a sudden happy realization followed: he'd *sung* the promise. That meant his words were binding, a promise made while nature listened. Such a vow even *he* could not break.

That meant Vane would most assuredly return in two days . . . he had no choice.

That also meant he could *not* come any sooner.

She would not be a prisoner of the house until his return. She could leave at any time without fear. She could visit to the alder grove and search for her broken solki.

She would visit Paavo.

And Jouko had two more days to find a way to free her.

Chapter Ten

Aino lay awake. Sanna slept beside her heavily on their straw tick. Aino envied the deep sleep, for a knot of worry in her stomach kept her awake. After Vane's sudden appearance, she'd withdrawn to her room, unable to eat for the rest of the day.

For the second night in a row, Jouko wasn't home. If he stayed away as long again, she'd be bound to Vane the next time she saw her brother. She'd considered sending word that Vane had given her only two more days, but she resisted. Jouko understood that the old man could show up at any time to claim Aino. No doubt, he was working tirelessly and as fast as he could to find a way to save her.

But patience became difficult to muster when her future hung in the balance. She ended up restless and scared. She yearned for the blessed oblivion of sleep but dreaded the possibility of nightmares. She'd had plenty of them the night before.

A horrid possibility occurred to her: What if Jouko wasn't still at Seppo's? Perhaps he'd been thrown from his horse and lay in the wood, alone and hurt.

What if Vane had learned that Jouko was trying to best him again, sought him out, this time stopping him for good?

Aino rolled onto her back and rubbed her forehead, unable to banish such worries so she could get some rest. Jouko could take care of himself. His songs would keep him safe. If he would sing to save his life, which she wasn't at all sure of.

And so long as Vane didn't find him.

She covered her face with her hands and stifled a groan. Fate seemed intent on destroying her life. If Vane didn't hurt Jouko, then he'd come get her anyway. Jouko would never uncover a song to free her because one did not exist.

I'm Vane's prize. She shuddered.

Perhaps there was a way to best the old man *without* magic. Could she somehow outwit him? The old stories spoke of the ground giant Antero Vipunen, who possessed secret magic about boatbuilding. If she could find him, if Jouko could learn that magic, he could build a boat to take them all away from Vane's reach.

No one knew where to find Antero Vipunen. Some said he spent his days in an underground grave, coming out only when he found a need or was somehow coerced. Even if she could find him, which would take far more time than she had left, she'd have to convince him to help her, which seemed about as likely as Vane cutting off his beard.

Aino didn't know how long she'd been staring at a shadow on the ceiling, abandoning one idea after another, when a knock sounded on her bedroom door. She sat up and held the bedclothes to her chest. A glance at Sanna showed her to still be deeply asleep. She snored, mouth hanging open slightly, her breaths slow and steady.

"Come in," Aino whispered.

The door creaked. Aino expected one of her parents to enter, but it was Jouko's unkempt blond hair that appeared in the doorway, lit by the moon as he slipped inside. His jawline had two days' growth of a beard that showed hints of red that matched her hair.

Aino gasped with joy and leapt from her bed to embrace him. He hugged her stiffly but gestured for her to return to the bed. Equal parts terrified and eager to hear his report, she sat on the tick beside him. Moonlight illuminated his face. She read no happiness in it. Fatigue lined his eyes and mouth. But she detected no signs of fear. Perhaps that was a good sign.

"Did you find a new song?" she whispered. Sanna would be unlikely to awaken even if the old man were to sing another storm, but Aino didn't want to wake their parents.

"Not quite yet," Jouko said. "I need more time."

"Is two days enough?"

"That's an awfully specific timeframe."

"Vane came today. He said he will come in two days. He *sang* it." Her voice was surprisingly calm.

"He sang it," Jouko repeated. "Oh, no." He brushed his hair out of his eyes with one hand and shook his head. "I suppose I should be glad he didn't take you today, but . . ."

Aino nodded. They both knew what the song meant; that Vane was bound to come when he said he would. She related the rest of the evening's events in the alder grove, including the demise of her solki. "We have two days. Less, I suppose, now. I *will* be his wife."

"This isn't right," Jouko said. "I wish we had more time."

"As do I." Aino worried the material of her nightdress between her fingers. She didn't want to hurt her brother by voicing her doubts, but a harsh reality lay before them—Jouko might *not* find a way to free her. Vane had easily bested him before, and he could surely do it again.

"You said you're getting closer. What have you learned?"

Jouko shifted to look at her more directly. "I found something theoretical, but if it's true . . ." He fished inside his pouch and drew out a torn piece of vellum. "I copied this from one of Seppo's books. Listen." He leaned to the side so moonlight spilled across the page.

Aino leaned in to read, praying that the words would provide a glimmer of hope.

"*Magic of any kind can be undone in two ways,*" Jouko read. "*Two ways only?*" He glanced at Aino as if to be sure she was listening, which, of course, she absolutely was.

"I thought there was only one way."

"So did I." Jouko returned to the page. "Listen to this: *The first method is most widely known: singing backward the charm already sung. The wizard who first uttered the song must reverse his own spell. Singing an enchantment in reverse returns the magic to itself, like rolling a rug.*" Jouko looked at Aino.

"Yes, yes." She nodded impatiently. "But what is the other way?"

Jouko read the next part quickly, his voice speeding up as his excitement built. "*Such is the only way a mortal singer can remove a charm or spell, but mortals are not the only beings who possess magic.*" He looked up at her with an expression that bordered on victorious.

The words had no application to her situation. "I don't understand."

Her brother's eyes sparkled as he read on. "*Immortals possess a different, more potent magic than that of their mortal cousins. Their magic can transform a mortal's enchantment into something else entirely.*" He excitedly tucked the vellum back into his belt pouch. "See?"

"No." Aino stared at him blankly. "What good is knowing about immortal magic? We don't know of any immortals. I already thought of getting Antero Vipunen's help, but that's a useless proposition. We are still in the same mess: unless Vane can be convinced to reverse his own spell, we cannot succeed."

"Didn't you hear? There *is* another way." Jouko grasped her arms. "Immortals can help us."

"Isn't Vane supposed to be immortal?" Aino wanted to believe, to hope, but didn't dare.

"He's half human, half immortal," Jouko said. "I don't know how that affects his magic. These last two days have taught me how much I have yet to learn."

She looked up at her brother with admiration, and not a little surprise. "Not too long ago, you would have sung a toad into anyone's boot who claimed you had much left to learn."

"Yet I do. I see now how little I know." Jouko lowered his chin and shrugged. "I pray I never again become so arrogant as to think I don't have more to learn." He took her hands in his and spoke with humility and energy. "Immortals are the key to freeing you; I am sure of it. They can change even Vane's enchantments, free you from his clutches."

A flutter of mixed hope and disappointment went through Aino. "But how?"

"I don't know yet, but I will study it out."

"Have you learned how to find an immortal?" Aino asked. "I don't know of anyone who has seen one in generations, and we have such a short time."

"I don't know. Nor have I discovered how to speak and barter with immortals or somehow convince them to help mortals." He heaved out a big breath. "Maybe it was a foolish idea."

Aino's heart dropped slightly, but she put a hand on her brother's arm nonetheless. The young man before her was not the selfish boy she'd known days before. "It wasn't foolish. Maybe there *is* a way for immortals to help us."

"You think so?"

"Yes. I've also wondered whether we can *outwit* Vane instead of *out-sing* him." So far, every one of her ideas had an obvious flaw, but Jouko was clever, and he thought like a singer. He might be able to find a weakness in Vane they could exploit for his undoing.

"Perhaps," Jouko said, rubbing his stubble. "I'll think on it tomorrow as I study immortals." He stood and headed for the door.

"Thank you, Jouko," Aino said. "For everything."

He gave a nod and a half smile. "I'll fix this. You'll see."

After the door clicked shut behind him, Aino rested her head on the down pillow once more. Would Jouko be able to help her? Could they find a solution—some loophole in the magic—to set her free?

Sleep continued to elude her as she imagined various tricks they might attempt to outwit the wizard. After a time, she sat up and pressed her hand against the wall at the head of the bed—Jouko's room lay on the other side. She imagined him in bed, staring at his ceiling pondering how to keep her safe.

She must have drifted off because the next thing she was aware, yellow-gray light of dawn filtered through the window shutters. It was light enough outside to seek out her lost solki, and she could do so without fear, since Vane couldn't come until tomorrow at sunset. She flung the covers to the side and climbed out of bed.

She quickly slipped a dress over her shift and tied on an apron, followed by an old leather belt, since her pretty metal one was broken and ruined, in pieces upon the dewy grass. She hung her embroidered pouch on the belt so that if she found her solki, she'd be able to put it inside.

After brushing the tangles from her hair, she wove it into one long braid, which she secured with a yellow ribbon. Then she opened her bedroom door and crept through the main room as quietly as she could. She could hear her father already out back, chopping wood. Sanna was still asleep, and Jouko's snores came through the wall. Her mother wasn't up yet, either, as she normally would be at this hour in winter to light the fire and thaw the ice in the water pail.

Aino wrapped a woolen shawl about her shoulders and slowly opened the front door. The heavy hinges creaked despite her efforts. She slipped through and scurried down the steps. She darted past the barn so her father, at the woodcutting block, wouldn't notice her and ask questions.

When she reached the alders, her step came up short. Just *seeing* the place again—the grass and foliage were still tamped down in the spots—made her middle queasy.

He can't come until tomorrow eve, she reminded herself. *I'm safe today.*

She dropped to her knees and searched the dewy grasses, ferns, mosses, and twigs for any sign of her solki. The latch would be lost forever, the tiny metal pieces reclaimed by the forest floor. But the main brooch could be fixed by a silversmith someday. She had to find the solki; losing it would feel like Vane had already won.

Her hands ran along the wooded floor, under ferns and around bushes and tree roots. She found not a glint of silver or color from the ribbons she'd thrown to the ground. Vane must have taken her rings, belt pieces, everything.

My solki. Her throat tightened.

Fingers outstretched, eyes straining in the early gray light, she searched and searched, and almost missed the tiniest glimmer of silver beneath a wild strawberry plant. She smiled widely as she reached under the leaves and retrieved her precious brooch. She wiped moist soil from the top with her apron and polished the surface before putting it into the pouch.

In the distance, the house door banged. "Aino!" Mama called. "Where have you run off to? You have chores to do."

"Coming." Aino clambered to her feet. She brushed the dirt from her skirts then closed the embroidered pouch with its wooden button. She spied the scarf she'd worn yesterday. She left it there. She'd never again wear it, not after it had been touched by his magic. She hurried back to the house, hoping she wouldn't be asked where she'd been or what she'd been doing. Explaining about Paavo and the solki would bring only more ire.

As Aino hurried up the outside steps, Mama grunted. "There you are. What, were you looking for your betrothed?" She laughed at her joke.

Biting her tongue, Aino ducked past into the main room. Her *real* betrothed lived a short walk away, and oh, how she wanted to see him. And to speak of him. To proclaim to her family that Paavo had given her a gorgeous solki as a token of his love. That her betrothed *wasn't* an old man who wanted her simply because she was young and pretty.

"I'll make the porridge," she said meekly, heading for the iron pot.

She measured the rice and barley and pretended that all was well. Aino put the lid back on the barrel and wiped grain dust from her hands. With her back to her mother, Aino felt her pouch for the reassuring outline of the brooch inside.

Chapter Eleven

When Mama left the house to draw water for cleaning the afternoon meal dishes, Aino withdrew the solki from her pouch. She unfolded a deep blue ribbon she'd found in the sewing basket and threaded it through the hole in the center of the brooch. The silver against the blue was striking, and while the result wouldn't be as wonderful as the original, it was still part of Paavo's gift. She'd never again let anyone take it from her. As her fingers traced the decorative lines, she wished she could wear the makeshift necklace visibly. She couldn't. Not until she was free of Vane.

The wooden steps creaked outside the door. *Mama.*

Aino quickly tied off the ribbon and slipped the makeshift necklace around her neck, hiding it under her dress. By the time the door opened, Aino had skirt, needle, and thread back in hand.

Mama came in and set down two large pails of water, and wiped her brow with the back of her hand. "I should send you girls out to carry the water. My back aches." She stretched and groaned then picked up the pails of water she'd drawn from the well and brought them to the cooking area.

"That's done, and the dishes can wait. Aino, come with me."

Aino looked up from her mending.

"Come." Mama waved her direction. "I have something to show you, remember?"

"What is it?" Aino asked. She set her needle aside a bit warily.

Her mother looked a bit too happy. "Come, come." She clucked her tongue and waggled her fingers for Aino to follow. "It's something special." Her eyes fairly sparkled.

Aino reluctantly followed out the door and down the porch stairs.

"This is so exciting!" Mama tossed over her shoulder. Her voice trembled with enthusiasm. Such a change in temperament could mean only one thing: whatever she had planned had something to do with Vane. Nothing else could possibly get her so worked up.

"Mama," Aino called to her back as they headed across the yard. "I don't want—"

"What *you* want is of no consequence." Mama whirled around and wagged a finger just as Aino opened her mouth to protest. "No. Not another word. I've been saving this for my daughters' weddings for years, but I lost it some years ago. Figured I'd never find it again. Now that I have a daughter about to be wed, I searched again and found it."

Aino had no idea what her mother referred to and had no desire to ask.

"Don't you think of ruining this for me. I've waited near twenty years for this day. Not even your father knows about what I'm about to show you. Come. It's in the shed." She picked up her skirts and scurried to the storage shed.

Aino followed to the very back, where the family kept items that didn't fit in the living quarters. She'd been here many times and didn't recall anything unusual. Only tools, feed, dried meats, onions, and other food, plus crates, stacks of cloth, a childhood doll, and a few books. Mama pushed and pulled several crates to the side to make enough room for Aino to stand beside her.

As Aino helped move crates and barrels, her mind went back to the same worries it had worked on ever since her talk with Jouko the night before—whether it was possible to outwit Vane.

What if today, she and Paavo secretly went to the tietäjä, the soothsayer and priest, and got married? Surely Vane couldn't insist on marrying another man's wife.

She obeyed Mama's order to heave one end of a blue trunk with white swirls and angles painted on the edges. When it was in place, she sighed. No, the village tietäjä would never perform a secret marriage; he'd insist on announcing the nuptials to the village at least two moons before the ceremony, as was tradition. He'd also confer with both sets of parents. Not to mention other traditions like the dowry, the ceremonial swords, the rings, the live animal offering . . .

No, a secret wedding was impossible.

Mama reached into a dark corner and gripped a leather handle. With a grunt, she pulled out a colorful trunk. Aino had never seen such an elaborate design—reds, blues, and yellows in intricate flowers. Aino couldn't help her curiosity from getting piqued—where had the trunk come from, and what was inside it? Mama wiped a layer of dust off the top and unlatched the lock.

An unusual sensation came over Aino, as if magic were inside the trunk. She could scarcely wait to see it opened. She quickly came to her senses and shook her head. Whatever was inside mattered nothing to her. Her circumstances would not be changed. She wouldn't be moved from her resolve; she would *not* wed Vane.

I will wed Paavo.

Perhaps they could run away and find another tietäjä. But no. If they were lucky enough to find someone willing to perform a marriage without any announcement, without many of the traditional trappings, marrying Paavo would put him in danger. Vane had been willing to kill Jouko over a silly challenge. He wouldn't think twice about killing Paavo to free her from matrimony. He could wed a widow as easily as a maid.

Mama rested her hands on the hand-painted lid. She paused before opening it, as if reconsidering. She turned around and sat on the lid, then clasped her hands together. "Before I show you what is inside, I must tell you how I came upon these treasures and why I had a singer from my home village put a protective charm on this trunk. You see, only I can open it. The spell ensures that no singer can even *find* it."

"So Jouko doesn't know about it either," Aino said as she comprehended what she heard. A charm had kept her from ever seeing the trunk before. "What treasures?"

Whenever Mama obtained anything of significant value, she showed it off to friends and eventually sold it when the family ran low on food. Why not sell this "treasure" long ago for food or clothing, if not for some frivolous things?

"Long ago," Mama began, "when I was yet a maid, I went berrying in the woods. I reached a hillside I'd never been on before, covered in the greenest grass and heaps of wild-flowers." She paused for a moment and bit her upper lip as if reliving the moment. Her usual abrasive tone had softened with the retelling. "The south side of the hill grew the darkest, juiciest raspberries I'd ever seen." Her eyes seemed to veritably sparkle in the dim light as she told her tale.

Aino leaned against a beam and folded her arms, determined to be skeptical regardless of the obvious shift in her mother's demeanor.

"I gathered a pail full of raspberries and wished I had a dozen pails, they were so sweet and plump. As I leaned over one last bush, I plucked a handful of berries and ate them." She seemed enraptured by her own story that she gazed into the air as if she could see the events like a dream before her.

"I heard sounds. They were strange and haunting, the likes of which I'd never heard. One was like a loom, and the other, a spinning wheel, only they were heavenly, like a song. The music came from somewhere nearby. I followed it to the other side of the hill."

She looked seventeen again. "The sounds were magical—tinkling and ethereal, not like the heavy, clunky noises of a wooden spinning wheel or the shuttle of the loom thudding back and forth."

Aino glanced at the trunk, half expecting some fantastic light to emerge from the cracks. "What did you find?"

Her mother might try to sweeten a story, but she wasn't imaginative enough to invent such a story. Both of them knew the reality of magic and could identify magical elements easier than most, thanks to Jouko's skills.

Mama stood and lifted her hem with both hands. She stepped in place as if reliving the moment once more. "I walked carefully, quietly around the hill," she said, her voice a near-whisper. "On the other side, I peered around a maple tree. At the base of the hill was a leafy grove, covered in the blue haze of the woodland. Through the haze, I saw . . ." She paused for effect and caught her daughter's eye.

"What?" Aino leaned close despite herself. "What did you see?"

"I saw the Moon Maid. She was weaving, and her Sun Sister was spinning. Together they made the most heavenly cloth for their gowns."

Aino had heard of the Moon and Sun Maids in childhood stories, but had never known of anyone who'd laid eyes on them. "What did they look like?"

"They were the most ravishing creatures I've ever seen," Mama said dreamily. "Their hair glistened like liquid gold and silver. Their robes flowed like water. Their eyes were as blue as the lakes."

"Did they see you?" Aino half expected to hear that her mother had been killed on sight, but, of course, she'd lived to tell the tale.

"They did not see me at first. I watched them, entranced with their beauty and song. But the longer I stood there, the more I longed to touch the cloth, to wear it, to have it for myself. I *had* to have that cloth." Her eyes flashed greedily, and Aino pulled back.

"I concocted a plan," Mama said. "I quietly stepped toward the grove, careful not to disturb their work . . . and I *spoke* to them."

Aghast, Aino felt her jaw open. Her mother had not only spied on magical beings, but she'd also had the audacity to approach and *speak* to them? Why hadn't they turned her into a pile of flax on sight? "What did they do?"

A satisfied expression smoothed Mama's face into a smile. She sat on the trunk again, her weight on one arm and her head off to the side as if she knew her words would impress. "At first, they did nothing—merely stopped their work and gaped at me."

As well they might.

"But then I dropped to my knees and clasped my hands." She slipped to the floor into the same posture. She looked heavenward at the rafters. "I beseeched them. 'Please, dear Moon Maid, give a poor young girl of your gold. Dear Sun Maid, give a starving girl of your silver. I am but a child, empty-handed, with only a pail of berries to call my own. I *implore* you.'" Her voice caught, and her face looked as if she might collapse in tears and die if she didn't get her wish. A moment later, the tragic tone and expression were gone. Mama hopped to her feet, wearing a smile that cut her face in half.

"Did they lay a curse on you?" Aino couldn't fathom any other result of such a display.

"They believed I was poor and in need of help." With an air of satisfaction, Mama folded her arms across her chest. "I'd worn my oldest dress and a frayed apron for berrying so I wouldn't stain my regular clothes. It was early morn, so I hadn't bothered to brush my hair. I surely looked a fright, all tattered and dirty. They took pity on me. The Sun Maid put a golden band around my brow and the Moon Maid adorned my hair with silver combs."

She touched her forehead as if she could still feel the gold and silver there, then sighed. "I wanted to ask for more— I still yearned to touch their cloth with a hunger so strong it overcame me. But they refused to part with so much as a tiny swatch."

Mama smoothed back her hair and sighed with contentment. "At least, they didn't part with any until a flock of geese flew overhead, honking loudly. With the Maids' attention diverted, I abandoned my pail, scooped up a gown in my arms, and ran home as fast as I could."

Her faced was flushed. She clutched her arms to her chest as if carrying the magical load and laughed almost maniacally.

Aino's curiosity turned to horror. "You *stole* a gown from the Maids?" She looked at the trunk and suddenly knew exactly what was inside. She took a step back to create more distance. "Why didn't they find you and strike you down?"

"Probably because their shock was so great." She laughed again. "No mortal had ever done such a thing before. By the time they thought of singing a curse on me, I was gone."

"But they could have still found you," Aino said.

"Which is why I had a charm placed on the trunk—to keep the them from finding the gown. Or our family."

No wonder not even Papa knew of the treasure. Taking the gown from the enchanted trunk would allow the gown to call to its creators. Then the Maids could find Mama and come lay a curse on the entire family.

Why did Mama think that removing the treasure would be safe to do now? Aino gaped at the trunk as if it were the greatest danger, a viper that would kill her if she drew too close.

"Oh, you needn't worry," Mama said, waving away her daughter's fear. "More than twenty years have passed, and the spell on the trunk has protected. The Maids haven't found me or the gown. I cannot imagine they still care about one simple dress, when they've surely made thousands more. They probably don't *remember* this one." She stepped forward and placed a hand on Aino's cheek. "Trust me. I've watched and waited. I've worried that I might be cursed, but nothing of the like has ever happened."

Aino wasn't so sure; their family had endured plenty of crop failures and illnesses, including one that took the lives of several babies born to the family.

Mama stepped close and took Aino's hands, which were now cold with fear. "I always knew in my heart that my daughters would be safe wearing the gown as brides, because neither of *you* took it. You are innocent. The Maids lack mercy, but they are just. They cannot hold you responsible for the dress. And just *think* how you will amaze everyone when you wear a gown that is beautiful beyond anything this village has ever imagined."

An idea began to form in Aino's mind, but perhaps it was all foolish fancy. If only Jouko were back from Seppo's. She could tell him her idea, and he'd have a far better understanding of whether it could work.

"I arrived home that day wearing the gown. I looked as beautiful as a flower," Mama went on. "Never had I seen such joy on my father's face. I looked ready to take wedding vows, of course, so at first he assumed I was betrothed to a wealthy merchant . . ." Her voice trailed off, and all happiness from her face turned to sadness. "That is, until he heard how and where I got the gown. Then he whipped me for such childish behavior."

"Oh, Mama," Aino said.

"After that, I put everything from the Sisters into this chest, then had our village singer charm the trunk—he never knew what was inside. Since that day, my treasures have been in this trunk here, waiting for a chance to come out and again adorn a young bride—a maid who *didn't* take them from the Sun and Moon sisters. You will wear them for your illustrious groom."

Aino had no intention of putting on a magical dress—or any wedding attire—for Vane. She didn't care what she wore to marry Paavo—her bridal gown could consist of a burlap sack if it meant they would be together.

Mama turned to the trunk and grasped the lid. Aino held her breath as the hinges creaked and the trunk opened. Gold and silver glimmered inside, and in the center, the most breathtaking blue cloth.

"There. Take the golden headband and the silver combs." She gestured but did not touch the jewelry in a boxed section. "And here is the blue gown woven by the Moon Maid herself and sewn by the Sun Maid's own hand." She lowered her voice as if seeing the gown for the first time. Or perhaps she'd forgotten how awe-inspiring it was.

"It's amazing," Aino said in a hushed voice. She could scarcely move her gaze; the cloth, the gold, the silver, all entranced her with their perfection. They seemed to glow with magic. Now she understood why her mother had taken the gown; Aino didn't know if she herself could have resisted such a temptation. At this moment, she longed to reach out and touch the shimmering blue material. To wear it. To call it her own.

No. The dress was stolen. It doesn't belong to me. She shook her head to clear it of the magic. The dress didn't belong to her mother, either. The Maids had been without it for a generation.

That time was more than half of Mama's entire life, but who knew what that time had felt like to the Maids? It could seem like no more than a few days had passed. After all, they were immortals.

Aino dared think more about her idea, as vague and immaterial as it was. Immortal magic could transform mortal magic. The Sun and Moon Sisters possessed immortal magic. Here in the shed, Aino had a connection with the Maids. If they still wanted their gown back, and she returned the dress to them, perhaps the they would be grateful enough to use their magic on her behalf.

111

How she would find the Maids remained the biggest gap in her plan, of course. A very big gap. No matter. She clung to the idea with every drop of hope her soul possessed, as it was the first possible solution she'd found.

"Put on the golden band," Mama said, reaching into the trunk.

Aino took the band, smooth and heavy. As she placed it on her brow, it seemed to meld itself to fit the shape of her head perfectly. It hummed with magic.

"And the silver combs." Mama did the honors herself.

Aino could hardly feel the combs; they had no weight she could detect, but the same rhythmic humming accompanied them, blending into a magical harmony with the golden band.

"Now the dress." This time her mother stepped away from the trunk. "I daren't touch what I . . . took."

Aino reached inside and withdrew the gown. It had spent two decades inside the trunk, yet the gown shook out with nary a wrinkle, flowing to the floor in gorgeous waves. Aino abandoned her woolen frock—which, in comparison looked coarse and pale—and slipped the dress over her shift. It molded to her figure as precisely as the band had fit her head. The magic surrounded her; Aino felt like the most beautiful woman in the world.

The dress makes me feel things that may not be true. And it isn't mine. The magic so easily muddled her mind and feelings.

The hum coursed through her with a song only she could hear. The dress called out to its mistresses, begging to come home. Aino nearly wept at the emotion.

Aino turned about. The hem swished against the floor as she spun. Her mother's face radiated happiness at the sight of her daughter bedecked like a bride.

"Oh, my sweet, you are a sight to behold."

"Do you think the Maids still weave and spin behind the hill you found?" Aino smoothed the skirt though it lay perfectly straight already.

"Oh, no," Mama said. "A year later, I went back to see—afraid that they might come for me. The trunk was safely charmed by then, but I still worried. They weren't at the hill. I checked again the next year. I don't think I could find them again, unless . . ." She gazed out the small window, where puffy white clouds played across the square frame.

"Unless *what?*"

If she knew why Aino wanted to know, she'd never say more.

"Unless I wear the gown again. While I wore it and before the trunk was charmed, I *knew* where the Sisters were. I saw them in my mind. I knew when they left the grove and went to a lakeshore. That's how I knew they weren't coming for me right away. They were angry with me—terribly angry—and I knew they had plans for revenge. I knew *which* lake they were at. I knew of the writ rock they sat beside as they sang their songs."

Aino tried to imagine a writ rock—an ancient stone with mystical writings carved onto its surface. She'd never seen one, but she'd heard of them.

"But that's nothing to us, is it?" Mama said, abandoning her melancholy tone as she pasted on a smile.

"No, of course not." Aino again smoothed the skirt with her hands, amazed at the perfect fit. The musical hum increased Again her entire body vibrated with song. She closed her eyes and listened. The dress sang to her mind again. As she listened, it was as if the gown, the band, and the combs told her where their mistresses were.

As she focused, Aino could see in her mind a huge stone that protruded into a lake like a small peninsula. No, not a lake. A larger body of water, though she couldn't tell how large. Right at this moment, the Sisters sat there talking with a maiden with green hair—a sea maiden.

They are at the seashore, Aino realized with a start. Marjala wasn't near the ocean. The Sisters were more gorgeous than Aino could have imagined.

Where on the seashore? She'd never been to the sea, she knew that the land there looked much like the lakes she'd been raised near—ragged edges, that went in and out and in again. The Maids could be anywhere along that massive jagged line that went mostly north to south, until it dipped to the east in a half-circle.

The dress immediately sang a new picture to her mind, moving from her family's small house through the woods westward as if she rode on a bird swooping through the air, on to the seashore. She saw the entire journey in three or four heartbeats but knew that the journey would take much longer.

I must hurry.

"You will be a stunning bride." Tears filled Mama's eyes, and she smiled with motherly pride. "Come back to the house. I'll finish dressing you so we can see what you will look like on your bridal day."

She took Aino's arm and drew her out of the shed, across the yard, and into the house. She disappeared in her bedchamber and returned a moment later with a wooden box. After placing it on the kitchen table, she opened the lid to reveal rings, bracelets, strings of green beads, and lengths of colorful silken ribbons.

"Sit, daughter."

Aino sat on the bench, and her mother lovingly adorned her with the contents of the box. Aino could not remember another time when she felt such love and warmth from those hands. For these few moments, she reveled in each tender touch as her mother's hands threaded braids with scarlet ribbons, placed rings on Aino's fingers and bracelets on her wrists. More than once she swallowed hard, worried that the solki would be discovered. But it lay smooth beneath her dress where the bulge should have been.

"There," Mama said after clasping a necklace around her daughter's neck. She turned Aino about and looked her over head to toe. "You will make me proud in that gown."

"Thank you," Aino said. "For everything." She hadn't meant to speak a farewell, but as soon as she'd said the words, she knew that's what they were.

She embraced her mother, clinging tight. Tears leaked out of her eyes, for she didn't know when—or if—she would return. Mama wouldn't understand, but this journey to the Maids must be done, and it could be done only while wearing their magical creations. They still sang to her soul, urging her to return to their mistresses.

Mama pulled away and touched the back of a hand to her damp eyes. "Wait until your father sees you. I'll put this box away, and then we'll go find him."

"I'll go find him myself," Aino said. "Perhaps he'll be in the fields and would like to see his daughter looking so fine." It was the best excuse she could think of to leave the house bedecked as she was.

"Wonderful idea," Mama said. "Why don't you bring his lunch to him? He'll never expect to see you like this." She scurried to the sideboard and put together his meal—a slab of dried meat, a piece of rye bread with butter, a small basket filled with strawberries, and a bottle of milk. She put them all into a bag and pressed it into Aino's hands. "Go, then hurry back to tell me what he says."

Aino held to the bag tightly. It contained what might be her only food for the journey ahead. She hoped her parents would forgive her for leaving without an explanation—but they wouldn't let her go if she gave them one.

Somehow, she knew that this was her only chance for freedom. She opened the door and stepped out then paused, looked back, and smiled.

"Goodbye," she said, then let the door shut behind her. She breathed in, feeling strength in the crisp air as it filled her lungs. For the first time since Jouko's challenge, she felt genuine hope instead of fear.

The old man couldn't come for her for another day and a half. And when he did, he would come to the family homestead; he wouldn't be looking for her west at the seashore.

She walked down the steps, threw a look northward toward Paavo's home, and spoke to him on the wind. "I will find a way for us to be together."

Chapter Twelve

As Aino left the house, her mother stood on the porch, watching her go. Aino turned around and waved, but her mother didn't go back inside; she looked too proud to see her daughter in wedding attire—magical attire, at that— to go inside quite yet. To avoid suspicion, Aino headed toward the field where her father was plowing. She walked along the wooden walkway he'd made. That kept the dress and her shoes free from any moisture or dirt. More than once she glanced over her shoulder, only to find Mama still at the door.

Aino had rounded a bend, went past the alder grove and several birches. At last she stopped and looked back to ensure that she couldn't see the house—and her mother could not see her, either. The highest part of the roof's pitch was visible, but only barely, nothing else—not the windows, the brown curtains, or the vases of bright flowers that lined the sill.

Aino lifted her skirts with one hand, the lunch sack secure in the other, and stepped off the walkway. Before picking her way through the forest, she let her gaze wander toward the field where her father was plowing. Could she risk a goodbye? If she were in her regular clothing, perhaps. Not dressed as a bride in the Maids' clothing, and not when she had only a little over a day to find them and undo the curse.

The humming from the dress and headband intensified, which broke her reverie and helped her return to the urgency of her task. She closed her eyes and let the music flow through her. In her mind, she saw the huge rock—nearly the size of a house—jutting into the water. There she could find the Sun and Moon Maids.

Her hand touched the base of her throat, where her solki yet rested beneath the gown. The brooch was a sign of engagement, and she stood in the wood adorned in the finest wedding attire. But she would be forced to be no man's bride—not today or tomorrow, at least, and never Vane.

Now that she was away from Mama's prying eyes, she wished to use a large pin to wear the solki on the dress, but damaging the Maids' liquid-blue cloth would likely offend them. She could not afford to do so.

Gods willing, her wedding day to Paavo would yet come. On that day, Aino would don a far less elaborate bridal gown, but she would far happier in whatever she wore. She tucked the hope into a small corner of her heart and returned to her mission.

She closed her eyes to help her focus, to speak to the dress. *Where are your mistresses?*

In response, the hem vibrated and emanated a glow, encasing Aino in blue light. Eyes widening, she twisted about to see behind her. Indeed, the entire hem glowed and pulsed with a glowing blue circle. But she received no image in mind, no words or instructions about where to go, where to find the shore where the Maids awaited.

Unsure what to do next, Aino faced front once more and caught her breath. A path appeared a few steps before her, lit by the gold band on her brow and the silver combs in her hair. Reverently, her hands reached up and touched them— they felt warm, and they trembled like tuning forks. She turned her head to the left, but the light didn't move with it. She looked to the right. Again, the golden-yellow and silver-white light pointed in the same direction as before. Southeast, she believed.

Feeling as if she was about to step into an unknown world, Aino lifted one foot and took a careful step forward. The light, a mixture of golden-yellow and silver-white, surely from the magic of the Sun and Moon Maids themselves, moved forward with her.

What about Paavo? She didn't take a second step, and she turned to face the path she normally took to his home. *I must tell him that I'm leaving. Jouko should know my plan too.*

No sooner had the thought passed than the glow ceased, as if someone had blown out a lantern. The contrast made the woods feel dark, like a winter night, rather than a typical day with shade from the trees.

Should I go straight to the Maids, then?

A slight hum warmed her, as if giving her permission to say goodbye.

Will you still guide me if I see Paavo first?

Another warm pulse.

May I wait for Jouko?

Nothing. No, more than nothing. Rather, the band and combs seemed to grow cold and stiff, as if it were winter.

I'll tell Paavo to inform my brother of my quest, and then I will leave.

The band and combs warmed and pulsed once more. A deep breath of relief came out of her like an emotional stutter.

"Thank you," she whispered, then turned the other way and rushed to the path that would lead her to Paavo's house. If Jouko hadn't been gone studying, she'd have told him, too, but she couldn't take the time to find Seppo's house. Her brother would understand.

Her skirts moved easily along the footpath, but walking with them—all fluttery about her legs, they were so light and airy—felt foreign. Constant worries of every kind plagued her mind. Would the forest floor, filled with moss, pine needles, and dirt, ruin the fine material? Would a dirty hem offend the Sun and Moon sisters? Would a slight tear from a rock or a branch make them less likely to help her?

Nothing she wore gave her any kind of answer, so she tried to think of her next step, of what she would say to Paavo, and not about whether the Maids would be furious and curse her before she could beg for their mercy.

She approached the Sorsa land through the deepest part of the wood and skirted it, staying where the pines grew thickest—in some spots, it was so dense that you could be but a dozen paces from a lake and not see it. If she stayed there, she could hide.

If any villagers spied her, they would grow suspicious; the gown and jewelry were far too grand for her family's station. They could force her home. One person could, for that matter, if it was someone like the wizened woodcutter, Matti. He was so strong that he could throw her over his shoulder like a sack of new potatoes and trot her to her parents' front step.

Worse, if anyone—villager or stranger alike—saw her, they could rob her of the gown and ornaments. Her cause would be lost, and she would be forced to wed the old singer. Hurrying to the sea and remaining hidden seemed two objectives entirely at odds with each other.

After what felt like the longest half-walk, half-run of her life, Aino reached the edge of the Sorsa home but hung back behind a wide tree. The last time she'd stood in this spot, Paavo had kissed her goodbye. She touched her lips at the memory—then worried about appearing without an errand from her parents as an excuse. That could be enough to raise questions, but being dressed like an elegant, wealthy bride would demand answers she was unwilling—and unable—to give.

Yet what choice did she have? If ever there was a time to risk revealing her relationship with Paavo, it was now. Imagining her courage tall and strong like her favorite spruces behind the family barn, Aino stepped from the cover of the trees and marched to the work shed. She gave the door two quick raps.

On the other side, a deep voice murmured, "Come in." A push on the creaking door let her into the dim room, where Paavo's father stood on the far side, focused on stretching a white fur on a frame. Paavo wasn't there.

"Mr. Sorsa?" she said quietly, from the shadows so that he'd be less likely to notice her attire.

He appeared to glance over in acknowledgement but didn't really see her. "Is that you, Aino?" he mumbled through the knife held between his teeth. He grabbed the blade, carefully trimmed something with it, and set it on the table beside him. "How can I help you? I'm plum out of reindeer skins, if your mother wants one. But if she's looking for another red fox pelt, I think I have one left somewhere."

"Thank you, but—" Aino's voice sounded high and foreign to her ears. "Is Paavo home? I need to speak with him." She felt every stitch awkward because of her elegant costume, as if he could hear the clothing's song and she meant to draw such attention.

Then again, did she hear the music, or did she *feel* it? She couldn't tell.

119

Either way, Mr. Sorsa didn't note the gown. Not for the first time, Aino was grateful for his distracted nature and the dim room he liked to work in.

"I sent him to check some of our traps past the bluff." Mr. Sorsa squinted through his glasses as he worked. "I expected him home by now, actually. But if we end up with an unusual number in the traps, he may not be home for some time."

"When would you expect him then?"

"Sometimes he spends the night and returns in the morning."

Aino's heart fell to her ankles. Waiting even a few hours wasn't a choice. "Oh."

"Can *I* help you with something?" He took his blade and scraped off a bit of leftover tissue from the back of the pelt.

"No, I . . . do you have a scrap I could write on?" She'd write a note and leave it in the oak tree where only Paavo could find it.

"Look in the box by the door," Mr. Sorsa said. As he returned to his work, he did a double take. He took off his glasses and looked at her closely, and his face wrinkled in confusion. "What is this?" he asked gesturing up and down with his glasses in one hand and knife in the other. "Getting married today, are we?" He laughed at his own joke—a wedding would be a great town event; they both knew she wouldn't be wed today.

Aino swallowed to wet her throat, which was suddenly as dry as sand. "It's my mother's. I have a question for Paavo about it." Truth, in a sense. And the closest to a complete explanation that she could give. With her mother's ribbons in her hair, Aino did look ready to stand before a tietäjä to be married. "Thank you."

She turned away quickly and retreated to the small pine table by the door. As she had hundreds of times a day since the duel, she prayed to the gods for help, this time that Mr. Sorsa wouldn't ask more questions or insist she return home. With each such prayer, she knew it might not be granted, and hoped that in this case, Ilmatar, would not side with her son.

I haven't been struck down by the gods, and I'm being led to the Maids.

Yet it would be better for me to be struck down dead than be forced to marry Vane.

She found a piece of leather about the size of her palm and turned to the small table, which was littered with leather-working tools and scraps of discarded hide. A bound volume of vellum pages that sat open with handwritten abbreviations, numbers, and totals. Finding a length of sharpened charcoal to write with took a minute.

As she sat down, she threw a quick look at Mr. Sorsa. He appeared engrossed in his work again. She set the lunch sack on the floor beside her and began to write.

Dearest Paavo,

I am journeying to find the Moon and Sun Sisters. I believe their magic is the kind we've been searching for, something that will allow me to break Vane's claim. I believe I have a way to find them and garner their help. The singer is coming for me in one more day, so I must leave now or risk losing you forever.

I will explain all when I return. Pray for me. Pray for us. Tell Jouko where I've gone. He'll understand and will be able to explain some of it. Show my mother the comb. She'll know where I went.

With all the love of my heart,
Aino

She folded the letter in thirds and then in half again, then slipped it into the sack.

"Thank you," she said, standing. "I'll go now. Give your wife my best wishes."

She hurried out before Paavo's father could ask what she'd written and for whom. After closing the door behind her, she rushed into the trees, heart pounding in her chest as she searched for the oak tree.

She searched and searched, certain she'd found it, only to be unable to find the trick door anywhere. She tried again and again, almost losing hope that she'd ever find it, so well had Paavo concealed the secret door—but she finally found the correct tree and the door. She reached for her knife to pry it open, only to realize she wasn't wearing her belt.

Praying yet again that the Maids wouldn't curse her, she withdrew one of the two combs from her hair and used it to pry the door open. It released without damaging the comb, at least from what she could see.

She placed the note on the box and placed the comb atop it. She closed the little door until it clicked and once more looked like part of the tree. Her hand rested briefly against the secret door before she turned her back to the tree and secured her hair with the remaining comb. Aino adjusted the gold band on her forehead. She smoothed her skirts, as if she needed to look her best for the Sun and Moon Sisters.

Now tell me where to find your mistresses. If you will but help me, I will bring you home after your long absence.

Golden-silver glow returned as bright as before, this time to her left. She moved that direction to follow, and again, and again, each step taking her farther away from the only home she'd ever known.

But, she hoped, toward a happy life. A life with Paavo.

A life free from Old Reliable Vane.

Chapter Thirteen

Aino followed the metallic glow through the wood. She turned left here, went up a rise and down into a valley, moving southward there, sometimes on paths. Mostly, she was led through untrodden ways, over groundcover, under groves, through swamps and meadows that looked untouched, as if no one had laid eyes on them in eons.

For the first several hours, she found the trip pleasant. The blue glow from her hem, combined with the gold and silver light from the band and comb showing the way, made everything seem ethereal. Several hours passed in which she nearly forgot the urgency of her errand and simply enjoyed being alone, with only nature and magic as her companions.

The day inevitably wore on, and her body grew achy and tired. Her mouth felt dry, eager for water. She ate the food in the sack, and then wild berries and strawberries along the way, yet her stomach ached, begging for more sustenance. The enjoyment gradually faded, and she had to urge herself to keep moving, to not stop. Whenever the temptation to rest came over her, she pictured Vane in the alder grove. His smug smile. His terribly thick muscles, which could wrestle a giant pike. His wrinkles, which testified of his age. His voice, so coarse that it sounded like two giant rocks scraped against each other. Those memories made her feet increase their pace, her legs lengthen their stride.

The sun began its descent, like a glowing cloudberry—and a reminder that her time for travel on this day was nearly gone. She had a light to guide her way through the trees. At some point, she mightn't be able to go on without rest, but she pushed on, fearing what would happen if she stopped. What if she intended to take a short nap only to find herself awake with the dawn? No, she couldn't lose so much time. She had to keep moving; she could already count the hours before Vane would try to claim her.

She increased her pace from a brisk walk to a light run. She shouldn't wear herself out altogether, or she'd collapse like a limp rag and be unable to go on. Yet she knew from the image of the shore that it was yet some distance away. If only she had a horse or a sleigh like Jouko used to.

Could she reach the Maids tonight? She doubted it. But if she tried to reach them in the morning, might Vane find her and spirit her away after all?

Light dimmed as the sun slowly dropped below the horizon. The air about her grew cool. She shivered, unable to stop looking askance at every shifting tree and bush, at every squirrel scampering across a branch or gust of wind sending aspen leaves aquake.

Vane can't come for me, not until tomorrow, she kept telling herself. *The magic won't let him*. Despite that knowledge, she remained alert and jumpy, and continued to grow wearier and wearier with each step.

At the sound of a cuckoo's song, Aino sucked in her breath and grasped the front of her dress. The volume wasn't the only thing that upset her; cuckoos were said to be connected to all manner of magic. Though Vane couldn't yet come for her yet, he could watch her, track her, by sending a spy in the form of a cuckoo.

Dressed as she was—glowing as the band, the comb, and the dress itself were—following her wouldn't be difficult. She forced her hands to unclench and relax at her sides.

She gazed upward, searching for the bird, but the search proved useless; the forest was too thick, with too many trees, to make out one tiny detail. The bird could easily have flitted from branch to branch, so she couldn't have seen it even if she knew where it had been. She lowered her chin and rubbed at the crick in her neck that had developed from constantly looking in the treetops and all around her for signs of Vane.

The glow of the gold and silver stayed strong, so she continued moving. The farther she went, the louder the humming became, as if the dress was antsy to be home after such a long absence. She could feel the words of the gown's song of celebration.

Sun Maid, spin your golden threads.
Moon Maid, weave your silver cloth.
Home at last, to you we come.
Home at last, to part no more.

The melody carried a hint of sadness with a quiet layer of triumph. The song nearly made Aino weep with sadness for what the gown had lost and cry with joy at the impending reunion. She wanted to fall at the feet of the Maids and declare her regret for her mother's thievery.

She sensed the Maids' sorrow over the loss, which ran deep and felt stronger than she would have ever suspected over what she'd assumed was one of hundreds or thousands of creations. Instead, the song gave her firsthand experience first of the anger and then the mourning the Maids suffered over what had happened when they tried to help a mortal.

Perhaps Mama was the reason no one had heard or seen the Sun and Moon Maids in a generation.

The sun slipped away, and the twilight gently drew night across the sky. Stars lit up the expanse, but no moon appeared. Aino could not recall what state the moon had been in when she left home. Had the Moon Maid withdrawn her light because Aino drew near with the dress? Or did this night simply have no moon?

The glow from the band and comb faded so gradually that Aino didn't notice until the light was altogether gone, and her foot caught a root. She stumbled and fell into inky darkness, catching herself on a low branch. She winced at scratches from spruce needles and bark and gasped for breath. She looked around, heart hammering against her ribcage.

Why had she lost the light that had guided her so far? Had she arrived? Without any light, she couldn't see far enough to tell if she was near water.

She might be hopelessly lost. Could the silver and gold have led her astray—to her death?

Nothing looked familiar. She could have been anywhere; the shapes of the tall evergreens, the ferns carpeting the ground, the lichen-covered stones, could be a minute's walk from her front door—or leagues and leagues away.

How far had she come?

How would she ever find her way home, when every direction looked the same?

She pushed herself back to her feet and touched the golden band about her brow. "Glow," she commanded.

Nothing.

"Glow!" she pled. "I do not know where to go next. Take me to your mistresses."

The band remained dark. She touched the silver comb, begged it for guidance, without success. She closed her eyes as she had when she'd first put the gown on and asked it to show her the way. Try as she might, she could no longer see the Sun and Moon Maids. She could not see the stone, the water, or the shoreline.

Every hint of her destination had fled her mind as if she'd never seen any of it. What to do next?

The band and comb had glowed so clearly before. Perhaps the gold band couldn't do so at night when the sun was no longer shined. But if that were the reason, the comb should have been dark in the daytime, without the moon.

Aino pressed her palms against her eyes, her mind hazy. She could not understand the magic at all. Smoothing her tresses with both hands, she peered through the treetops and searched for any sign of the silvery orb. Thousands of stars twinkled like pinpricks, but no moon.

Her head throbbed; she tried to ease the tension by rubbing her temples. *I don't know what to do now.* Her mind felt too weary, too muddled, to think. Every bit of her body ached, protesting how much she'd asked of it.

She reached out for the trunk of the tree she'd used to help herself up, sure she would collapse to the ground without more support. Even as her eyes adjusted to the dim light, the forest remained so dark that she could see naught but vague shapes of trees.

But there—there in the distance, between some of the dark lines that had to be trees—she spotted something. A movement. A sparkle.

Water? Tears sprang to her eyes. She took a few steps closer, gripping branches to keep her steady. Her feet snapped twigs and crunched dry needles, but she paid them no heed; how could she, when she'd finally reached the sea?

At last Aino came to an opening in the trees. She stepped onto a sloped rock, and the enormous sea glittered before her. It extended farther than she'd have believed possible. To her right, a rocky outcropping stretched from the shore into the water—the very writ rock she'd seen in vision.

But no immortal sat upon it.

Had she been led astray by the magic? Had everything she wore—the band, the comb, the dress—all conspire to show her the wrong path? If so, why? As punishment for a crime committed years before Aino's birth?

She tried to remain strong, but her mind, her heart, and her body had given all they had. Fear and dread seeped into her bosom without resistance. Utterly spent, heartbroken at her failure, Aino lowered herself and lay down on a bed of pine and spruce needles, no longer able to care whether the gown remained pristine.

The Maids aren't here. My time is almost gone. I'll die here.

As she drearily gazed out over the ripples of water, her stomach gurgled. Her stomach felt hollow.

Perhaps I'll starve here. The possible outcome occurred to her without emotion. She could not care any longer. Every drop of emotion had been wrung from her.

As night went on, all she could see was the undulating surface of the ocean and the starlight reflected from it. She closed her eyes, not because she wanted to sleep but because her lids refused to stay open. In her mind's eye, her family appeared.

Would Sanna cry when her little sister didn't come home? How soon would Jouko hear that she'd gone? Mama would be furious, no question, but likely more over losing the old man as kin than losing her youngest child. What would Papa think?

How long would Paavo mourn her? She didn't want him to be sad forever.

Forgive me, she thought to them all.

At last her body wilted, and like the dress, now stilled into silence, Aino felt herself drift into unconsciousness, unsure if she would ever return.

Chapter Fourteen

"The thief! She's returned."

"We'll not let her escape again."

The two female voices woke Aino with a start. As she lifted her head from the pillow of moss she'd rested on all night, she opened her eyes. The early light of dawn slanted sharply, so she shielded her face with one hand, unable to see the speakers. They sounded angry, but at the same time, their voices had a musical quality of such beauty that Aino would have been happy to listen to them all day even if they remained angry.

A melodic grunt of annoyance, and then, "Look. She has soiled the hem."

The mist clouding Aino's sleepy mind made thinking hard, but when her memory of the previous night returned, it came in a rush. She remembered in a rush where she was, what she wore, and why she she'd slept near the seashore, on a forest floor far from home.

The Sun and Moon Maids. The realization should have thrilled her, but she felt chilled to her core. She sat bolt upright and turned in all directions, but found no one. The voices *had* been near. Had she imagined them?

"Hello?" Aino called. No answer. She slowly got to her feet, her achy body protesting every tiny movement. "Where are you? Who are you?" Still no sign of anyone. Not another melodic word. "Are you the Sun and Moon Maids? I've come to find you." She held up the hem of the dress—now covered in mud, as one of the voices had said with utmost disdain—and took a few steps along the rocky shore. "Sun and Moon Sisters," she called to her left, her right, even above her, "My message is urgent."

"Why should we listen to a thief?" The sharp question came from directly behind Aino. She whirled around with a gasp.

Then, at the sight of the figure before her, she felt bathed in awe. The woman could be none other than the Sun Maid. Radiant in gold, she stood not four paces away, her arms folded, one bright eyebrow raised in challenge.

Aino couldn't think or speak. She could scarcely breathe. She hadn't been prepared to see such perfection—flawless skin, eyes the color of amber, hair undulating about her shoulders as if there were a wind only she could feel. Her gown seemed to be pure, golden sunlight wrapped about her curves. Aino could feel the heat the Sun Maid radiated and had to resist holding her hands out as one would to a fire to get warm.

The gown burst into song much more loudly than ever, and this time, the music and words were audible to her ears as well as to her mind.

Mother, mistress, we are home.
Take us in your loving arms.
Please watch o'er us; that we be
Nevermore to lose our way.
Nevermore taken away.

The Sun Maid's hard mouth softened into a pleased smile. "Yes, dear, you are home." Her eyes traveled to the neckline and sleeves; her gaze felt like a weight. "My sister and I will keep you here forever, my love. We have learned to never trust a mortal."

At that, her gaze snapped to Aino.

"I—I—" Aino stammered. "I am not the thief."

"Do you deny wearing the gown I made with my sister?"

"No," Aino said hurriedly. "This is your gown, but I didn't steal it. My *mother* did."

The Sun Maid regarded Aino suspiciously. She tilted her head back and folded her arms.

"Truly, I am not the thief." Would the Sun Maid believe her? Have pity on her? Or would she curse Aino? The fact that she was still alive, that the immortal hadn't killed her right off, gave her some hope that the Maid could be reasoned with.

"Why are you here?" the Sun Maid demanded.

"To return the gown my mother stole. To right her wrong."

The Sun Maid took a turn about Aino as if summing up her character. "You do bear a striking resemblance to the girl who took the gown."

"I have been told I look like my mother did when she was young," Aino offered meekly. "She's much older now."

The Sun Maid passed behind Aino and rounded her from the other side. "Yes, I suppose that as a human, she would have aged." Her eyes continued to trail up and down Aino's frame.

From farther into the wood, the other voice spoke. "She made a grave decision."

At the sound, Aino nearly stumbled on the loamy earth. Consumed as she had been with the Sun Maid, she'd forgotten about hearing two voices.

"She committed a *crime*." The Moon Maid appeared between two trees. Aino had no idea if she'd simply not seen the Moon Maid before, or whether the Maid had only now materialized.

The Sun Maid stopped before Aino once more. The Moon Maid hovered nearby but remained in the shadow of a tree. Her silvery dress moved like waves of water and sparkled like crystals. Aino tried not to let her beauty—equal to or possibly slightly greater than that of her sister—tie her tongue.

She cleared her throat and looked from one Maid to the other. "You must believe me. I didn't take your gown. I came to return it."

Gods, help me explain.

"My mother hid the gown from you with a charm. Only yesterday, she dressed me in your clothing in preparation for my nuptials. I'd never seen the gown nor heard of it before that. I came as quickly as I could." Would that be enough to satisfy them? She should have decided before now what to say and how to say it.

The Moon Maid made a single movement that was more a glide than a step. She came farther into the light, where Aino could better discern her features—shimmering skin, blue eyes with silver pupils. Her arms were now folded strongly across her chest, a twin to her sister's posture. "Did your fool mother send you on this errand? Does she hope her daughter will ingratiate herself with the Maids—and steal more treasures?"

"Oh no. She didn't send me." Aino shook her head rapidly. "I came on my own. I traveled all the day and did not sleep until I no longer had a guide, and it was too dark to see."

The Sun Maid glanced at her sister. "And what does she think of this journey of yours?"

Aino hadn't thought that far until that very moment. "She will be most upset. I wouldn't be surprised if, when I return, she casts me out of the house and never speaks to me again." The knowledge made her chest ache.

The Maids exchanged wary but less hostile glances. The Sun Maid tilted her head. Locks of gold spilled across her shoulders. "You must forgive us if we do not believe that your motive is entirely altruistic. For what other purpose have you come to us?"

"You must have one," the Moon Maid added.

They were right, of course, but Aino again didn't know what to say to avoid their wrath or to gain their help. She stood there, struggling to speak to immortals, when a week past, she hadn't believed they existed. Yet her future—her very life—depended on their willingness to hear and aid her cause.

The Moon Maid drew nearer. The Sun Maid did the same. The Sisters were so close that Aino could have reached out and touched them—if she'd dared. Instead, the Moon Maid lifted her arm and drew a finger down Aino's sleeve, tracing the flawless weave she'd made twenty years before. Her face softened as she remembered happier times, but it quickly hardened again. "Tell us. *Why* have you come to us? Do not waste our time. What do you want?"

The Sisters waited in heavy silence for Aino to answer, but at first, she couldn't find her voice. She daren't ask for favors after dredging up painful memories for the Sisters. Their stern expressions sent her middle rattling like chicken bones in a sack.

"I searched you out because I want two things."

"As we suspected," the Moon Main said.

131

"Leave, foolish girl," the Sun Maid added with a dismissive wave. The Sisters turned on their toes and walked away.

"First, I wish to return your stolen treasure," Aino called after them.

They paused in their step. Then the Moon Maid turned about and tossed over her shoulder, "Do you really think we couldn't just take the gown?" She inhaled deeply as if preparing to sing, so Aino rushed on.

"Allow me to right my mother's wrong."

The Moon Maid let out the breath and exchanged looks with her sister, who turned about now as well.

Aino removed the silver comb and gold headband and held them out. "Take these, too. I don't have the second comb with me, but I know where it is and can fetch it."

The Sun Maid rolled her eyes. "Do you think us so foolish as to withdraw a gift offered in good faith? If you do, then you do not know magic."

They were right, of course; she didn't know magic well. "Oh, I see." She replaced the comb and band.

The Moon Maid nodded her agreement. "It is the cloth we spun and wove, the gown we labored on with our hands and our hearts, the dress taken from us so cruelly, that we desire to have again. And we have every intention of taking it."

"I'll give it to you now." Aino moved to slip an arm out of the sleeve.

"Now?" the Moon Maid said, clearly surprised that Aino was about to give up the gown of her own accord. "Girl, stop."

Aino froze, her arm only halfway out of a sleeve. The Sisters put their hands out, palms forward, and opened their mouths to sing.

What magic would they make? Would they punish her? Take the gown and leave her in nothing but her shift? How would she get home? Would she have anything to wear?

"Not yet!" Aino called before the song could start. "May I ask for the second thing before you sing?"

The Maids laughed sharply, bitterly. The Sun Maid spoke first. "Have you not heard us? We are finished helping mortals."

"Even if we were to agree," the Moon Maid added, "why would we help the child of a thief? Look what it wrought last time."

"On the other hand, Sister, she did return of her own volition," the Sun Maid said. "Let us hear her request."

"Very well." The Moon Maid sighed. "Speak. What is it you want of us?"

Aino measured her words. She had no need to explain who Vane was; he'd lived long enough for the Maids to know. Because his mother, Ilmatar, was Goddess of the Air, some people said he was immortal, but Aino knew otherwise. He aged, and even the stories revealed the fact that he could be wounded and fall ill. Best to begin with the curse.

"I want to break a bind that ties me to Vane."

The Sun Maid took yet another step closer. "Old Reliable Vane?"

"Yes," Aino said, tensing at the nearness of the immortal. "He is to take me for a wife today. This because of a contract my brother foolishly entered into."

Today.

The word made the curse feel far more real that she'd allowed it to seem before. If the Sisters didn't help her, this would be the last day of her life as Aino, the farmer's daughter. From this day forward, she might be Aino, wife of Vane. This was her last sunrise as a free maid. Last night was her last sleep free. She shuddered.

"How are you bound to the singer?" The Moon Maid didn't challenge Aino's claim of being bound and seemed more curious than suspicious.

Aino told the whole story from the first moment she saw Vane at the market to Jouko's note about immortals' ability to transform mortal magic. "Can your magic save me?"

The Sun Maid jutted her chin out. "Our magic can save you from the hands of that miserable man. *That* isn't the question."

"The question," her sister went on, "is *whether* we'll help. We don't like thieves any more than we like Vane."

Aino wanted to protest—again—that she wasn't the thief.

133

"Besides," the Moon Maid added, "I don't know what good it would do us."

Suddenly, the Sun Maid, hereto the more sullen of the Sisters, chuckled. "Seeing Vane bested would provide me much amusement." She laughed again. Her golden dress rippled. "He has always thought far too much of himself, don't you think?"

"Upsetting him would be grand," the Moon Maid agreed. Her eyes sparkled with mischief, and she smiled as broadly as she could with her lips closed. "He's been arrogant and patronizing ever since that encounter with the reindeer last winter."

Aino didn't care why they helped, so long as they did. She looked from one Sister to the other. "Oh, Vane will be most cross if you free me."

"Yes, I believe we will help you." The Sun Maid looked positively joyous. She looked to her sister for confirmation, and the Moon Maid grinned her approval.

"Oh, thank you!" Aino's heart soared with relief; she felt as if she could fly. She wished she could embrace the sisters. "I cannot express the depth of my gratitude."

The Moon Maid raised a hand, cutting off Aino's effusion. "Before you thank us, you must know *how* we can help."

Did that mean the immortals' magic couldn't undo all mortal spells?

"We do not break or reverse human spells," the Moon Maid said. "We *transform* the type of enchantment that already exists into something else."

Aino looked from one Sister to the other. "But you can you free me of Vane's claim?"

The Sisters looked at each other again as if having a silent conversation only they could hear. The Sun Maid spoke next. "We can certainly keep you from his clutches. We'll make sure he won't find you today or tomorrow."

That sounded like almost everything she wanted. "What about after tomorrow? Can you stop him from finding me forever?"

"Not exactly," the Sun Maid said. "But we can make sure that he cannot marry you."

Aino didn't know if her mind spun in circles from fatigue, hunger, or the Maids' riddles. "Will I be free of Vane's claim?"

The Moon Maid reached out and stroked Aino's hair with an unexpected sympathy. "No," she said. "None but Vane himself can do that. When he renounces his claim through song, you will be completely free."

Just as quickly as relief had washed over her, despair crashed down. "But he will never renounce his claim." She fought the tears threatening to choke her throat.

"He may yet," the Moon Maid said, "when he realizes he cannot marry you."

"But—" Aino began.

The Sun Maid interrupted. "Do you want our help to escape Vane's clutches?" she took Aino's arm in her hand, which was so warm that she nearly cried out from pain. "Speak now, before you weary us."

"Yes," Aino said. A tear escaped one eye. "I want to escape Vane's clutches."

The Moon Maid fingered Aino's hair; her cool skin sent a shiver through Aino.

The Sun Maid touched the slight bulge under the gown—Aino's solki. The brooch became immediately hot. Aino gasped at the intensity, but tried not to draw back, as to not offend. The Sun Maid drew the solki out of the gown and studied the design.

"Quite pretty," the Sun Maid said. "Would you like to keep it after you receive our help?"

"Oh, yes," Aino managed. "Very much. Please."

"We can arrange that. Come."

She beckoned. Aino followed the two Sisters toward the huge, shimmering body of water. She hurried, watching for tree roots and stones so she wouldn't trip.

They walked past a reedy marsh that edged the shore beside the stone outcropping, which looked almost like a small peninsula. The rock was identical to the one Aino had seen in vision the moment she'd first donned the gown. They stepped onto the outcropping, which was fifty paces long and half as wide and narrowed as it went the farther from the shore.

Seawater glistened under the morning sun but lit up more as the Sun Maid passed.

They stopped near the far end of the outcropping, several paces from what had to be the writ rock. The columnar stone was rough cut and stood waist high. It bore a multitude of carvings Aino recognized as magical and sacred, though she didn't understand them.

The Sisters had walked to the writ rock and now stood there, staring out to sea. Aino didn't know what to say or do, so she merely raised her head bravely and waited.

After a moment, the Sisters spoke to each in other in whispers. At last, they turned to her.

"Remove the gown," the Moon Maid ordered.

Silently, Aino complied. Within moments, she wore only her shift, the solki around her neck, the gold band, and the silver comb. She held out the gown.

"Drop it," the Sun Maid said.

"On the dirty stone?"

"Drop it. Now." The Sun Maid looked in no mood to be questioned. The levity the Sisters had shared moments before had vanished.

Aino obeyed, gently lowering the gown to the stone rather than dropping it in a heap. Then she stepped back, waiting for the next instruction, determined not to speak again until asked to.

The Sun Maid gestured toward the carved stone. "Sit."

Aino eyed the Sisters anxiously and walked to the writ rock. What would happen to her when she sat on it? Would it be considered sacrilegious and anger the gods?

She hoisted herself up to the rock and clasped her hands in her lap to keep them from shaking. Her knees knocked against each other, so she crossed her ankles and pressed her heels against the rock in hopes of remaining still.

"Look," the Moon Maid said.

Aino followed her gaze and made out three elegant figures jumping from the water and diving back into it, slicing cleanly through the surface. They drew closer with each leap. At last, Aino recognized them as creatures she'd heard of but never laid eyes on: sea maidens. One had blue hair, a second green, and the third was flaxen-colored. They climbed from the water, colored hair draped across their shoulders like seaweed. Water dripped from their scanty clothes.

The green-haired sea maid spoke first. "Hello, Moon Maid and her Sun Sister." Her voice sounded like bubbles.

"Good morning," the Moon Maid said. The Sun Maid nodded in greeting.

The flaxen sea maiden looked between the Sisters and Aino. "Are you busy?"

"You may watch," the Moon Maid said. "This will take only a moment." The Sisters smiled, extended their arms palms up.

This is when I am made free.

The sea maidens' eyes seemed to swim with sea water. Their beauty entranced Aino, so she pressed her eyes shut to better listen to the Sisters' song—one that was sure to be soothing and, as Mama had said, haunting.

The first three notes were tinny and disjointed and sounded much like a knife scraping a tin cup. Soon Aino couldn't breathe; she forgot about the pretty sea maidens and all else. All she could do was gasped for air, but none filled her lungs.

At the same time, her body shook and pulled inward, as if something pressed on her from all directions. Panic engulfed her.

They're killing me!

She tried to get off the writ rock—to flee, but could not move at all. She still could not get in any air. The Sisters sang on, arms outstretched, their voices sounding strange and twisted. Unwillingly, Aino's head moved back, and soon she was staring at the sky. The world seemed huge, growing and expanding all around her.

She tried to stand, to kick, to somehow escape, but it was as if she had no arms or legs at all. She flopped to her side and could only look straight ahead. Why hadn't she fallen off the writ rock? She could still feel it beneath her, beneath her entire body. The rock had expanded with the rest of the world.

Or have I shrunk? She struggled to make sense of how the world continued to change.

The writ rock shifted, lowering into the stone outcropping. Down, down, down. At the same time, the seawater rose, but far too fast to be the tide. The water lapped against Aino as she still lay on her side, first touching her eye, then the front of her face, and then most of her body. At least, she assumed the water must have reached that far; she could no longer feel her arms or legs.

She gasped for air, her mouth opening and closing uselessly. She tried to close her eyes to shut out the pain, but they wouldn't move.

I have no eyelids, she thought with a start. *What happened to them? What is happening to me?*

An echo of her own voice reached her mind, as if one of the Sisters answered her query: *It would be better for me to swim with the fishes in the sea than to be an old man's comfort.*

She'd said those very words. Aloud.

With horror, Aino realized that they were becoming reality. She tried to move, to stop the song, but all she could do was flop about and flail her tail and fins.

The Sisters' song continued. Aino still could not breathe. The Moon Maid nodded toward the blue-haired sea maiden, who went to Aino and, with her thin, wispy limbs, picked her up in one hand, giggled, and hurled her toward the sea.

Aino sailed in an arc through the air. She landed with a harsh splash in the cold, salty sea. Once more she flailed, but quickly quieted when she could breathe again. She swam under the surface and tried to gain her bearings, figure out what had happened. Yet she knew.

I'm a fish. A fish!

She tried to look at her body but couldn't bend enough to see herself. She no longer had a neck. As she moved through the water, she sensed her fins and tail. They seemed to know what to do.

This cannot be.

She swam in circles, breathed with gills, and had fins. In disbelief, she peered up through the water. The Sisters stood on the outcropping, which was no longer immersed. The writ rock stood beside them at the same height, as if it hadn't just sunk to lower her into the sea. The Maids grinned at each other, then at Aino below them, clearly pleased with the effects of their song.

The Moon Maid caught Aino's eyes and grinned with satisfaction.

They promised to free me. To keep me from Vane's clutches. Instead, they . . .

As quick as a flick of her tail, comprehension opened her mind. The Sisters had indeed kept their word. Aino could not marry the old man. He would not find her today or tomorrow.

I'm cursed. Miserable, Aino rotated her fins to stay where she was, to watch the Maids. *They kept their word; they transformed the magic, exchanging one prison for a different kind. They have given me a living death.*

The three sea maidens swam around her, their blue, green, and flaxen hair flowing with the current. "Welcome," the flaxen-haired one said, her voice high and fluid.

The blue one swam in a circle around Aino, which pulled her attention from the shore. The sea maid pointed. "What is that below your mouth?"

Aino had no way to speak to them. No hands or arms to gesture with. Not so much as shoulders with which to shrug. Her confusion must have shown on her face somehow because the blue maiden pressed, "Your scales there are most unusual."

The green-haired maid twirled in the water. "Yes. They almost look like a circle, but there's more."

"Looks like flowers and berries," the flaxen-haired maiden said. "How strange."

Aino shivered with a thrill. The Sisters had kept another promise in a most unusual way. Her scales bore a likeness of the solki.

"Come explore with us," the green sea maid said. She dove downward without waiting to see if Aino followed. She didn't.

She floated in the water, fighting equal parts terror and fury—the former over her future and the latter at the Sisters.

Could they have not turned me into a sea maid, at least? Did they think the likeness of Paavo's solki would make me happy when I can't see it?

Aino would have wept if she could. Instead, she slowly swam away from the outcropping at the writ rock. Her tail swished side to side in the water.

Chapter Fifteen

Jouko slaved over stacks of books—memorizing, writing notes, cross referencing, following a thread of a theory only to abandon it and pull his hair.

A knock sounded on the library door, but he ignored it. The door creaked open, and someone stepped inside—not Eva. He looked up to see his father there, his face covered with a sheen of sweat from a hasty ride.

"What is it?" Jouko asked, standing so fast he nearly knocked over a stack of books. "Has he come for her already?"

Papa shook his head. "Not yet."

"Then why are you here?"

"Your mother needs to see you. She's unwell."

Jouko looked at the desk, filled with vellum and texts and notes. He shook his head. "I can't leave now. What ails her?"

"She's just unwell," Papa said.

Jouko had a sense that Papa would be equally vague with any question. "I'm sorry. I must stay awhile longer." He sat again and scooted his chair in.

"Aino is not home to help, and neither are you. Sanna acts like a scared puppy when your mother yells, which I cannot blame her for—"

"Papa," Jouko interjected. "I must stay her as long as possible. This is about far more than living with Mama's temperament. This is about your *daughter*."

"You don't understand what it's like." Papa's face reddened, and he gripped his hat between both hands. "I *cannot* abide your mother's ailments alone."

"Well, you must," Jouko said, turning back to the desk. "I will not come now."

Without warning, Papa crossed the library's threshold and tried to physically drag Jouko outside. The two nearly came to blows, but in the kitchen, Jouko finally escaped his father's clutches and managed to get, the table between them. He had no desire to hurt his father.

Papa ran a hand across his eyes. He looked haggard. "Son. Come. Now. I beg you."

"No!" Jouko planted his palms on the table. "You cannot expect me to abandon my work in the final hours I have to save Aino! How can you not see that I do this for her?"

"But this *is* about Aino," Papa said.

"How?"

"Just come home."

"Soon. Not yet." Jouko had never crossed his father before, and doing so now felt like a betrayal—but not as much as abandoning his sister would be. "Later."

"When?" Papa's angst-ridden question pulled Jouko out of his anger. "When will you come home?"

Jouko looked out outside and eyed the angle of the sun. "Not too much longer. I must be home before dusk, when Vane will arrive."

"Then I will wait." Papa went outside and sat on the stump used to split wood.

For a moment, Jouko felt guilty, as if he were the cause of his father's sorrow rather than Mama's uncontrolled moods. He pushed away the feeling and hurried back to the library, where he closed the door. Until the sun had moved farther across the sky, his work was not done.

But the time flew past, and all too soon, the weight of failure descended upon Jouko's shoulders. If he left on his horse now, he'd get home shortly before the sun began to drop into the west. And he had no more clues about how to save Aino than he had before.

He put the texts away in their proper places, including the old volumes into their secret box. Eva could lock it for him after he left.

Dejected, he accepted a quick embrace from Eva before meeting his father outside. Soon the two of them rode toward home. His father still refused to say more about Mama and in what manner she was unwell. Jouko didn't press for an explanation. With every clop of his horse's hooves, he wished he were back in the library, with books of magic around him. For the first time in memory, his studies had yielded him absolutely nothing.

He ground his teeth with frustration and wondered how he could have found more time to research—perhaps he'd spent too much time over meals with Eva. What if an extra ten minutes would have yielded the information he needed?

Whatever her ailment is, I won't be singing it away. He assumed it was her recurring stomach pains and headache, likely both. By now, the family knew he refused to sing; he'd refused to help in ways he used to—stoking the fire for supper, removing a splinter from Sanna's finger, and easing the pain of a dying lamb.

The next time he sang, it would be to free his sister from Vane once and for all. If such a song did not exist, then Jouko would die without ever singing another note, no matter how many years he lived.

After they reached home, they dismounted. Papa reached for Jouko's reins. "Go inside. See your mother. I'll take care of the horses."

Jouko surrendered the leather straps. "Remember, I will not sing."

"We shall see," his father said. "Now go. She needs you."

After a sidelong look at his father, Jouko went inside the house. Unsurprisingly, Mama lay on the wood couch, propped against pillows. Sanna sat at her side, dabbing her brow with a damp cloth.

"My son! He's back!" she called, holding out a limp hand.

"What is the matter?"

If she hadn't been known for theatrics, he might have spoken with more sympathy. She groaned and pulled Sanna's cloth to her forehead. "Oh, the pains of motherhood! Do they ever cease?"

With raised eyebrows, Jouko turned to Sanna. "What has happened?"

Sanna dipped the cloth into a bowl of water then looked at the floor, avoiding his face. "Aino is gone."

"She's *what?*"

Mama wailed. "Oh, my head! My heart!"

In a few quick strides, Jouko reached her side and lowered to one knee. He gripped his mother's hand. "Has Vane taken her already?" That seemed impossible; the oath forbade him from coming until later that evening.

"We don't know where she is," Sanna said. "She just left." She finished with a helpless shrug.

Rapid footsteps pounded up the porch, followed by a hard rapping against the door. "Is Jouko home? I must see him," a familiar voice called from the other side.

Jouko crossed to the door and pulled it open to reveal Paavo, who looked paradoxically pale with fear and flushed from exertion. He leaned his hands on his thighs to catch his breath. In one hand, he clutched a piece of folded leather.

"What is it?" Jouko asked.

Paavo's sudden arrival had something to do with Aino. Jouko had observed enough to guess that the two cared for each other as more than neighbors. But was his news good or bad?

He stepped onto the porch beside Paavo and closed the door for some measure of privacy. If Mama's illness was real this time, rather than her usual hysterics, extra stress might stop her heart altogether. If she had concocted this ailment, as she so often did, Jouko had no desire to deal with added cries over her suffering.

"Aino left me a note." Paavo wiped a sleeve across his forehead. "It makes no sense to me, but—"

"What does it say?" Jouko's attention fixed upon the scrap of leather in Paavo's hand.

"She's gone to find the Sun and Moon Maids."

"Who?" Jouko asked.

"The Sun and Moon Maids," Paavo repeated. "She says they can save her."

Jouko searched his memory and barely remembered hearing stories about the Sisters. As a boy, he'd preferred tales about wizards, not immortals.

Immortals! Of course. Aino must have decided to find immortals to reverse the spell.

143

But how did she choose the Sun and Mood Maids? He stepped off the porch and began pacing to and from the path leading to the road. Dozens of troubling questions swirled in his head.

On his way back the second time, Paavo stopped his movement by holding up the note. "Listen to her own words."

Jouko looked over his shoulder as Paavo read the note aloud.

> *Dearest Paavo,*
>
> *I am journeying to find the Moon and Sun Sisters. I believe their magic is the kind we've been searching for to break Vane's claim. The singer is coming for me in one more day, so I must leave now or risk losing you forever. I will explain all when I return. Pray for me. Pray for us. Tell Jouko where I've gone. He'll understand and will be able to explain some of it.*

"*Do* you?" Paavo turned quickly, moving the note out of Jouko's view. "Do you understand it?"

"But you didn't finish."

"Do you understand it so far?"

"In part, yes." Best to explain so he could learn what else his sister had written. "I found an old text that says immortals can transform mortal magic. I don't know what that means, exactly, or how it works, or a thousand other things. The text has missing pages and is written in an old dialect. I searched that volume and the rest of Seppo's library, but didn't learn anything else useful." He sighed. "I just shared a theory with her. Aino must have been desperate enough to flee in hopes of—"

"No," Paavo said sharply. "She would never leave, alone and without supplies, because of a *theory*."

"You're right," Jouko said simply. "She wouldn't just flee." The sister he knew made deliberate choices. She didn't rush off blindly on impulse.

Like her brother.

"Somehow," Jouko said, "she has found information about the Sun and Moon Maids, including how to find them.

I'd bet my voice on it." He gestured toward the note. "Read the rest."

Paavo nodded eagerly and held up the note. "There's just a little more. *Show my mother the comb. She'll know where I went.*"

"What does our mother have to do with anything?" Any clarity from a moment before vanished.

"She left this with the note." Paavo withdrew a decorative hair comb from his pouch.

"Is that real silver?" With a touch of awe, Jouko plucked the comb from Paavo's outstretched hand and rotated it from one side to the other, admiring the intricate workmanship. He'd never seen the like. "Where would she have gotten such a treasure?"

"I don't know," Paavo said. "But apparently, your mother does."

"That's right," Jouko growled. He wrapped his fingers around the comb. He ran into the house, where Mama still lay on the couch, moaning.

"My dear girl, missing!" she cried. "How could she abandon me? Such selfish behavior toward the woman who gave her life."

Jouko shoved the comb under her nose. "Where did this come from?"

The moment his mother saw the comb, she sat bolt upright, and her face drained. Her hand darted out to take the comb, but Jouko yanked it beyond her reach.

"Is she dead?" Mama cried. "Did you find her wearing it? Vane will be here soon, and—"

"Where did this comb come from, and why did Aino have it?" Jouko's expression became a fierce scowl. "*Where* did it come from?"

Her air of tragic sadness transformed into one of feigned innocence. "I have no idea." She smoothed the comforter on her lap again and again, deliberately avoiding Jouko's stare, but her trembling hands belied her calm voice.

"Help me find your daughter." Jouko knelt beside her the couch and reined in his temper. "I beg you. No more lies. Tell me about the comb."

Mama shook her head. "I daren't speak of it." She shut her lids tightly, sending tears down each wrinkled cheek. Her mouth tightened into a knot. After a minute of silence, she opened her eyes to see him, still waiting expectantly.

"Tell me," he said calmly but firmly.

She covered her face with both hands and wept. She rocked back and forth, but Jouko didn't relent. After further coaxing, Mama spoke. "I fear I cursed my daughter. The comb was a gift I received long ago from the Moon Maid." She ignored Jouko's wide-eyed shock and went on, dry washing her hands. "The Sun Maid gave me a gold band for my hair. I was greedy and wanted more." She stared at her lap but didn't go on.

"Oh, no," Jouko said. A heaviness came over him like a cloak of lead. "*What* did you do?"

She covered her eyes with one hand. "I stole one of their gowns."

"No," Jouko breathed.

"I've kept the gown and trinkets in a shielded trunk for twenty years. I hoped to help Aino find happiness in her upcoming nuptials and be dressed fit for her groom. So, I dressed her in the gown and the combs and the headband. You must believe that I only wanted her happiness."

How is it that everyone believes they can control and decide Aino's life except for her? Myself included. In fact, myself foremost.

"What are we to do?" she wailed. "The day is almost spent; Vane will arrive at any time. What will he say when she's not here?" She was nearly frantic as she grabbed Jouko's shirt with both hands. She pulled so hard that he had to lean down. "What if he's vexed to find her missing, and he kills us all?"

Anger simmered in Jouko's chest—at himself for getting the family into this mess, at his mother for wanting Vane as a kinsman. At Aino for running away into who knew what kind of danger.

"Vane will no longer bother us," Jouko vowed. "I started this, and I will end it."

"How?" Mama asked at the same moment.

"Yes, how?" asked Paavo, who must have entered during the discussion.

Jouko didn't answer them. He walked out of the house without a look back, but he said one sentence over his shoulder, loud enough for them all to hear. "I'm going to kill Vane."

At this, Mama threw the blanket off her legs and ran after Jouko, who was halfway to the storage shed by the time she reached him.

"*You* can't kill *him*," Mama cried, with apparent new strength, as she began to run. She gripped his shirt in her fists once more. He pried her fingers off then yanked the shed door open. "Don't you remember? It's not been a week since he nearly killed *you!*"

"Oh, I remember. Trust that I'll remember the duel to the end of my days."

He stepped inside the dank shed alone, to the wall where he kept his hunting supplies. One hook held his crossbow, and beside it, rows of hooks holding his three best arrows. Before his apprenticeship, he'd been a skilled hunter, with aim better even than Ari, the champion elk hunter. After Seppo's tutelage, Jouko made these arrows with the aid of song. They'd never flown astray. If he could not best Vane with song, he'd best him with true aim. And if song helped that aim, so much the better.

He tucked the arrows into his belt and lifted the crossbow from the wall. It felt natural in his hands, like an old companion.

When he emerged from the shed, Mama yet stood outside. She gasped as if she hadn't believed him in earnest. "Have you lost your wits? Remember where your pride got you before—up to your neck in a swamp."

"I must act. Not for my pride, but for my sister's very life and freedom." He turned to Paavo and clapped a hand to his shoulder. "I will do all I can to bring my sister back to you."

"Thank you," Paavo said. "You're a good man."

The statement felt untrue; Jouko didn't know how to respond to it. He wasn't so sure that he was a good man at all. He'd been proud and selfish, and now he was trying to right a terrible wrong of his own doing. Did a good man ever create such a wrong in the first place?

He hefted the bow's weight, felt the contours of the wood. It had always shot true for him. Would that it remained so today.

He walked into the forest and selected a solid tree with several rows of branches he could use for climbing. Halfway up the tall pine, he perched on a thick branch. The vantage point gave him a good view of the road to their home as well as the stretch of road the old singer would almost certainly arrive by.

Jouko eyed the sun almost ready to set. The sky had turned scarlet and orange. The singer would come soon. Perhaps he was deliberately waiting until the end of the day to heighten the family's anticipation. He could still hear Mama's sobs and wails in the distance, followed by Paavo's quieter, soothing tones.

After some time in a cramped spot on the tree, Jouko's back grew stiff, his arms heavy from the weight of his cross-bow. He stretched his neck and looked west. The last rays of the sun had dipped below the horizon. The air cooled fast now, making the hairs on Jouko's arms rise like gooseflesh.

Still no sign of Vane.

The singer had to come before nightfall; he was bound to do so with the song he'd used the last time he'd visited. Jouko kept his ears trained to hear the slightest hint of en-chantment, perhaps of Vane conjuring snow.

Instead, he heard hooves clopping along the packed dirt road, but without magical song. Could it still be the old man? Jouko leaned toward some branches to better see the road. A large yellow horse and rider moved rhythmically, drawing ever nearer. At first Jouko could not identify the silent rider.

Best be careful. He nocked an arrow, focused his aim, and waited. Soon he knew all too well that indeed, he'd found the wizard; the bushy beard and tell-tale pouch with the Braid of Fate was all the evidence Jouko needed.

Before he released the arrow, Mama ran into view, screaming, her hands over her mouth. Jouko breathed out in frustration and lowered the bow.

"Honorable Vane, give us time to find our wayward daughter!"

The old man's horse kept its pace, forcing her backward. When Vane reined in his horse, he stayed in the saddle—and sat directly in the bow's line of sight. Once more, Jouko raised the crossbow, aimed carefully, and let an arrow fly. The twang was too quiet for the old man to hear at this distance, and the arrow, which Jouko had crafted for stealth, sailed silently through the air. But then it veered sharply to the ground and slid noiselessly into the grass below the horse's belly.

Jouko narrowed his eyes. Was his aim poor? Had the old man surrounded himself with a shielding spell?

"My wife-to-be is not here?" Vane said, voice echoing through the trees.

Mama visibly quaked. As she spoke, her voice cracked. "She ran away, sir, unbeknownst to the family. But she will still be your wife. Give us time."

"My tietäjä is waiting for us at Vane's Knoll. He is ready by a stone altar of my own with everything needed for the ceremony. Do not trifle with me, woman." His deep voice rumbled, making Jouko unsteady on his perch in the tree. He clenched the crossbow tighter.

"Please, have mercy and be patient with us, a poor family," she begged. "We need time to gather a proper dowry, and we don't yet have a groom's sword. But my daughter *will* be found, and she will be yours." She fell to her knees, hands clasped, tears rolling down her cheeks.

For once, Jouko was glad to see his mother's vivid emotions; perhaps this one time, they would help someone besides herself. He put another arrow in place. This time he aimed slightly higher. He released the catch, and the arrow, flew. It sailed high and to the right, and land in a bush. A shield had to be warding Vane.

No matter. Jouko had magic too.

"I will search your farm for her." Vane's face turned a dark red. "For your sake, I hope she'll be found hiding inside a flour barrel." He clucked his tongue and dug his heels into the sides of his horse. Mama scurried out of his way.

Jouko had little time; soon the horse would be out of sight. Under his breath, he sang a charm he'd composed long ago under Seppo's watchful eye. The song called forth precision in making his arrows fly true.

149

He added an additional progression to send the arrow through the shield. He held each note precisely, remembered the right words in the right order, Jouko released the arrow.

At first it flew straight for Vane's back, but at the last moment, when it reached the shield, it veered slightly to the right. Instead of impaling Vane's barreled chest, it found its mark on the horse's flank. The horse whinnied in pain. It kicked and thrashed, trying to free itself from the lance.

With his three arrows spent, Jouko cursed and slammed the now-useless crossbow to the branch before jumping to the ground in one leap, a three-note melody softening his descent.

I must free Aino. Vane's death was the thing that would clearly break the man's claim on Aino. *Gods, help me kill him.*

Jouko raced across the forest floor toward the road, with a singular goal in mind—kill the old man quickly. The frustration over his final arrow missing its mark boiled up, but Jouko forced it down. *Think,* he demanded. *You cannot afford to be distracted. Think!*

The horse continued to buck and kick. Vane had been taken off guard enough to have lost hold of the reins. He scrambled to reclaim them and not fall off the saddle.

Apparently, he is a better sleigh driver than horse rider.

The steed flung its head up and down in violent swoops. The animal bucked again, this time Vane lost his grip and fell.

Jouko seized the moment. Before the old man hit the ground, he sang a deep, sure note that held Vane suspended in the air. Jouko's song wound Vane's scarf around his head, making sure to cover his mouth before knotting the ends. Thoroughly gagged, Vane couldn't sing a counter-charm.

Jouko's next song flung the old man into the sky. Vane flew higher and higher into the air, his arms and legs extended like crossed laces. The charmed wind carried him higher and higher, then westward, toward the sea.

The longer the song went, the more success Jouko had with it, the stronger his confidence grew. His volume increased, and he walked onto the road, where he could see Vane's shrinking figure, the better to steer his course. The song gained power with layers of melody, braiding itself into a form of magic Jouko hadn't known was possible.

Rare, magical words and phrases returned that he'd learned only days before in the secret volumes. No matter that he'd only seen them once and never sung them; the words came to the forefront of his memory and out of his mouth.

Mouth bound, Vane made muffled noises of disdain, but he couldn't sing. He couldn't move his arms enough to pull off the scarf to free his voice. He drifted up, up, into the skies, arms and legs moving as he tried to gain purchase.

Note by note, word by word, Jouko sent him farther away. He added notes to enhance his vision so that despite the dimness of the evening, he could see the old man well enough to keep the magic aimed directly at him. He pushed the wind, singing Vane farther and farther away. At last, even with enhanced sight, Jouko could no longer see the wizard's beard or his ruddy coat as more than a dot in the distance.

"You did it!" Paavo's voice came from somewhere. He gave Jouko a congratulatory smack on the back, ending the song abruptly with a note all but swallowed in his throat.

The spell cut off, and the dot that was Vane dropped. Jouko considered singing again, but knew he needn't. Vane was far enough away to be well over the thick forest. He'd land in a mess of treetops, where he'd meet his death among branches.

Watching the speck descend did not make Jouko happy. Relieved, perhaps. Oddly, the fact that he'd finally bested the most lauded singer in the world didn't give him satisfaction. He no longer sought the admiration of others. All that mattered was his sister.

Now that the danger had passed, a heavy breath escaped Jouko. "I'm . . . weak." His knees felt like rice pudding. Sweat rolled down the sides of his face from the exertion of singing the most important and complex song of his life. He wiped his forehead, his entire body weak from the effort.

"Come." Paavo slipped an arm under Jouko's for support. "Lie down. The old man is dead. Aino is safe."

⁂

Vane fell from the sky. Cold wind rushed past him. He'd been flung far from Aino's home. The boy had greater power than he'd assumed. But despite the boy's intentions, Vane did not fall to his death.

The moment the young man's song cut short, Vane felt it. Life and strength returned to his body. His limbs had control once more. He ripped the scarf apart, freeing his face. He gasped for breath and had to look about to get his wits about him.

And then he sang.

His voice lacked its usual power, but it slowed his descent all the same. Instead of plunging into the treetops, he drifted on the air like a feather. He noted the ocean in the distance and floated that direction. There, he landed on the water as gently as a babe placed onto a blanket. His powers had returned in full. Floating on the water, he lay back, put his hands behind his head, and sang himself to shore.

Foolish boy, he thought with a chuckle. *Your sister will still be mine.*

Chapter Sixteen

A ino swam and swam. For how long? Possibly days. It could have been hours. Or weeks. She didn't remember and had no way to track time. Not even the lightness or darkness of the water helped. Darker water could mean that it was night, or simply that she'd swum deeper.

For the moment, the sea was light, and as she swam about, she saw object beyond the water. This time, at least, she knew that it was daytime, and she was near the surface.

The sea maidens wouldn't answer her questions about time or the ocean or anything else. Their attention would not be diverted from lighthearted play, and Aino quickly tired of their games. The sea maidens cared for nothing but jokes and tricks, and she couldn't play along. All she could do was swim around them and envy their arms and legs, their ability to stretch, to touch things with fingers, to do somersaults in the water, to kick, to laugh, to cry.

Aino's fish form could do little but move side to side, up and down. She ate bugs and smaller fish when she was hungry. They never tasted good, and didn't satisfy for long. She ached for the luxury of sleep and wished for a soft place to lie down and rest her eyes. Yet even that wish felt like a dream; she had no distinct memory of tasty sausages and potatoes, of slices of pulla flavored with cardamom, of resting on a soft bed, and closing her eyes.

They remained open, always. Hadn't they always been so?

Yet wisps of memory, of a life before kept returning—a life that resembled the sea maidens and yet felt entirely different. One word kept appearing in her mind: dry.

She couldn't remember what *dry* meant.

She heard something, not a sound, but a feeling from inside her, one with words. *Swimming with the fishes would be better than life as Vane's wife.*

What did that mean? Had she spoken those words?

Another image returned—an old man with a thick beard. A man who wanted her, but not as a fish. A man she had to escape. She shivered, sending tremors through the water.

Whoever the man was, she sensed he wanted her as his prisoner. That life would be worse than the one she had in the water. At least, she believed it would be worse. Maybe, after more time here, she'd feel differently. The more she pondered on the threads of memory, the more of them came to her, as if she pulled on a thread of yarn and unraveled the past, drawing pieces of it to her one strand at a time.

Suddenly she yearned to chew bread, though she couldn't recall what precisely that meant.

What a joy it would be to warm my hands at the fire, to stitch with a needle. Yes. More and more of her past life returned to her. *I would give much see my brother again. Jouko. That is his name. And Paavo! Oh, to be held his arms.*

The thoughts tumbled about in her small brain. Each felt translucent and transitory, as if they would vanish if she didn't cling to them hard enough, and perhaps she'd forget again even then. Next time, maybe forever.

If only she could cry, the pain might lessen. But fish couldn't shed tears. She swam to a patch of seaweed and burrowed within it. The shadows kept darkening her simple mind and wounded heart. In the clump of seaweed, she knew instinctively that soon, she'd forget about her human life altogether.

Thinking at all had already become a chore. Sinking into the oblivion of instinct was so much easier. Yet surrendering to that very forgetfulness might be a grace bestowed from the gods to protect her from misery. Never again would she know joy or pleasure. Never again would she know pain, either.

She watched schools of fish swim past, the individuals within them as unthinking as the one before and after. They mindlessly moved as a group. Yet they were content. She envied them.

A length of something fell into the water. A string, per-haps? The word felt right, but she couldn't be sure. Whatever it was, it hung straight with a piece of wood at the end. A part of her mind that was still human cried out that this was a danger. That the sharp points on each end of the wood could kill her.

A juniper lure. That's what it was. She remembered.

A herring from one of the schools came to investigate.

"Go away," Aino tried to yell, but her voice sounded like muffled streams of water. She tried again, this time swimming out from the clump of seaweed, between the lure and the her-ring. "It's a lure. It will kill you."

The green and silver fish paid her no mind. It didn't un-derstand her words. It likely couldn't comprehend death, or grasp what a lure was. The herring was dumb of mouth and simple of brain. It swam around Aino and closed in on the lure. Its tail moved back and forth with grace. But then it opened its mouth and tried to eat the piece of juniper. The whole lure went into the mouth, sharp points and all. The her-ring swallowed. Suddenly it jerked to and fro, trying to escape. The string above them tightened. Aino looked up and made out the forms of fishermen on the shore, excited over their possible catch.

The fish twisted and flopped about, its tail moving fran-tically, all in a vain effort to get free. Was the herring's reaction emotional, or purely instinctual?

In the end, the answer didn't matter. The inevitable oc-curred: a wooden pole from above was drawn up, and the fish rose with it.

Aino looked away. She remembered what happened next. While human, she'd caught and prepared many fish— salmon, herring, and whitefish. So many times, she couldn't count. She'd cut them open. Cooked them. Eaten them. None of that had ever seemed any more meaningful than a simple chore.

But now she was one of those simple creatures of the water. Watching them get caught felt like murder.

As quickly as her body could go, Aino swam from the shallow waters, as far into the salty ocean as she could, but no matter how long she swam, she could not escape the image of the doomed herring, flailing as it rose to the dry world above, where it would die.

The same thing could happen to me if I lose my sense of humanity. She could fall prey to a juniper gorge or some other lure. She tried to think of something other than her possible death by fisherman.

What if my sister were to swim in the sea and brush past me?

What if Mama one day washed our clothing in this water?

The worst thought kept returning to her tiny brain like a fist against a thick, wooden door.

What if Papa or Jouko catches and eats me?

She swam in circles faster and faster, hoping to get dizzy enough to rid her mind of such morbid images. It didn't work. Once more, she swam away from the shore, and when she was far enough that she felt safe, she turned about. In spite of the note she'd left behind, Paavo and her family would never know what happened to her after she set off to find the Maids. They would all assume she'd died, while instead, she swam in the cold, miserable sea.

I'm more than a fish. I can still think. I can speak. If I can find someone who can understand me, I could get a message to my family.

This was Aino's first glimpse of comfort. She'd given up on the idea of ever regaining human form, but if her loved ones could know what had befallen her, she might be less miserable. But who could she speak to? She had yet to find any creature in the water who could understand her. Yet she felt certain that when she spoke, genuine words with meaning came out.

She'd need to find a person. And that would require being close to the shore, where the fishermen lay in wait. After some time debating the risks of fishermen and lures, she decided to swim over. She reached the shoreline and swam along it, looking up every so often in hopes of seeing someone she could talk to.

The water here was warmer here than in the deeper areas, and the color seemed bluer. This close to the surface, she could tell that the sun had fallen into the horizon, and night was fast approaching.

I've been in the water for at least a day, she reasoned, not recalling another sunset since her transformation. *Months could have passed, and I would not know it.*

But no. I still have my wits. I can't have been here so long as that.

She stopped swimming near the reeds that bordered the outcropping. The writ rock still stood there as it had when she'd first sat upon it as the Sisters transformed her. Of course, there was no sign of the Sisters or the gown she'd returned. For a moment, she wondered if she'd imagined it all—if she'd ever been human.

Movement on the shore near the trees caught her eye. Through the water, she couldn't make out the shape, only enough to tell that the figure was short. A human child? Aino poked her face out of the water to get a better look. She'd expected to be unable to breathe, but somehow, putting her face out of the water didn't suffocate her. The realization was oddly terrifying; if she were to be fooled by a lure, she wouldn't necessarily die a quick death.

The shock of being able to breathe slowly cleared, and Aino remembered why she'd poked her face above the surface to begin with: the movement in the distance.

There it was again. She made out tall ears. Big, fur-covered feet. Only a hare.

She almost slid back into the water, when she heard muttering. She lifted her head higher and listened carefully. Yes, she definitely heard words. Not a song, but someone complaining under their breath.

"Send me off to find blueberries after the sun has gone down. Those women think I can be ordered around because of who they are, do they?"

The speaker appeared in a gap between the trees, and Aino's fish mouth opened slightly in surprise. A magical hare. She hadn't known such a creature existed.

Aino tried calling the hare before it hopped away. "Help!" She was so excited that the word took much of her strength; she had to drop back into the water to rest.

The hare's ears snapped up, and it cocked its head in Aino's direction. After a moment of looking curious, the hare jumped onto the stony outcropping once, twice, a third time, its nose twitching, eyes searching the water. Aino's tiny heart hammered. She poked her head through the surface again.

"Do you understand me?"

The hare started and pulled away. Its head moved up and down, but Aino couldn't tell if the hare meant to answer her question or was simply behaving as a hare did. She tried once again.

"If you can understand me, please speak."

The hare rubbed is paws together as it scrutinized her. "I can speak and understand you. How can you speak? You're a fish."

She might have asked the same of the hare. "I'm really a maid who asked the Sun and Moon Sisters for help."

They *had* helped, in their own way, but certainly not in the manner she'd hoped for, or in any manner she could have dreamt up.

The hare snorted and shook its head. "Another rescue in the form of a prison, eh? The Sisters are quite good at that."

"Yes, that is it exactly." Aino couldn't help but flit to and fro in the water; she hadn't felt this alive, this human, since her transformation. "I didn't ask them to be a fish."

"I guessed as much," the hare said with a roll of his eyes.

"I only asked to be free from wedding the wizard Vane."

The hare drew closer, eyes narrowing. It leaned down to her, and spoke. "Are you the maid Aino?"

He knew of her! He would believe her, maybe help her. Her fins beat the water into a flurry.

The hare stroked the fur on its chin. "The woods have been singing your story on the winds. Truthfully, the Maids don't know the difference between a blessing and a curse. They don't mean to be cruel, I assure you. As immortals, they don't understand."

"How do you know so much about the Maids? My brother is a singer, and I only just learned of them."

"I know them as you do," the hare said. When Aino twirled and settled into the water—her way of sighing now— he nodded. "Indeed. Once I was known as Kari the Tietäjä. I called on the Sisters to save me from a sinking ship and certain death." He made a sad noise that was half-chuckle, half sigh.

"Because the powers of a tietäjä come from the underworld, I've never feared death. I've come very close to dying many times, and always came away with my powers strengthened, with great visions, greater understanding."

"But not that time," Aino said soberly. She understood far better than anyone else could. "And the Sisters saved you."

"Yes, they saved me from drowning." Kari held out his fur-covered arms. "But look at me now. While I didn't drown, the existence they damned me to is worse than if I had and been sent down to Tuonela. At times, I long for death." He pulled his long ears as a man might rake through his hair with his fingers, then turned as if to leave.

"Wait!" Aino called. Her tail splashed the water to one side and then the other, disturbing the water's surface.

The hare turned back and, without a word, waited for her to continue.

"Kari, could you tell my family what's befallen me? They must think I'm dead."

She sensed that she needn't explain more, that the hare knew much of her story, as it was already spoken of on the winds. He might know why she'd left home with the Maids' clothing, about the contract to become Vane's wife.

The sun had disappeared until morning, and a handful of stars twinkled in the sky. The sight sent an odd sense of victory through her. The day Vane had sworn to wed her had come and gone. Though he could still claim her, he'd failed in his original goal. She tried to smile at the realization, but her mouth opened only up and down.

He glanced toward the woods, askance, then back at Aino. He didn't speak, but he didn't leave, either. That fact alone gave Aino hope—and helped her hold fast to the memories of being a woman.

"Please. Tell my family of their lost daughter. They live in Marjala, about a day's journey east." The conversation had sapped her strength. Aino dropped her scaly body into the water to rest as she awaited an answer.

Kari eyed her warily. More than once, he glanced surreptitiously into the darkness of the forest. After what felt like an eternity, he nodded. "I suppose delivering a simple message won't anger the Sisters . . . much. If I return to them with their berries before I go, they can't complain. Helping you won't interfere with their magic, at least not directly."

She swished back and forth anxiously, lest speaking a word would destroy her odds.

"Very well, I'll go." he sighed. "Your family will receive the message."

Aino took a deep breath so she could hold herself above the surface again. She raised herself up and said, "Thank you, sir. Thank you!"

The hare nodded in acknowledgment and hopped away. Weary but at peace, Aino swam slowly, aimlessly. Her family would know. When Jouko learned of her state, he'd tell Paavo. Perhaps her mother would learn once and for all to stop meddling in matters that did not concern her. Perhaps one day, Jouko would find a way to turn her back into a human and keep her free from Vane at the same time.

Or perhaps not. Both were unlikely, and even more unlikely was the possibility of Jouko finding her. Such a rescue was far too unlikely to justify nurturing so much as a seedling of hope.

At the edge of the shore, the hare stopped and turned back. "Farewell, Aino," he said. She resurfaced in time to see him. By the light of the stars above, she sensed him smile. He twitched his nose and then hopped away in long, easy jumps. Soon his pale fur was lost to her sight.

She floated in the saltwater, her tail and fins barely moving. Now that her family would no longer wonder, her fate didn't matter so much. She let the current carry her. Her mind gradually became muddled as it had before.

If she turned into a mindless fish fooled by an old fisherman's lure, so be it. At least Paavo and her family would know that she'd left them to fight for her freedom, never surrendering to Vane's demands of marriage.

Darkness crept over the landscape as confusion crept over her fish mind. Soon her mind blended into indistinct swaths of color that made no sense.

Vane's demands. Marriage. The words flitted across her mind, but they no longer held meaning.

The water is cool and fresh. She enjoyed the easy life of the sea.

Chapter Seventeen

Jouko sat on a log near the family sauna, a pile of birch cuttings beside him. He worked to make the vihtas for that evening's sauna. For days now, he'd been anxious and weary, but he found work with his hands to be soothing.

Odd to have forgotten that tasks like this one could be enjoyable, even preferable to accomplishing them with magic.

Mama and Sanna were already in the sauna. While he didn't want to rush them, he anticipated his turn, to feel the heat surround him, gently melting away all aches and worries. He had yet to fully celebrate the fact that he'd bested Vane at last—something he wouldn't have believed of himself only a few weeks ago. How could he celebrate without Aino home, safe and well?

His one happiness lay in the fact that when Vane died, the wizard's claim on Aino died too. All that remained to set things right was finding her and bringing her home. In the morning, Jouko would pack supplies and head out on his horse, due west, as she'd gone. He wouldn't return without her.

And I will find her safe and well. His worry to the contrary, however, revealed itself when he pulled the ends of the twine so hard that the birch cuttings bent, nearly splitting some altogether. The resulting mangled bundle seemed to mock him. He'd made sauna vihtas for years, since he was a boy, but had never ruined one like this.

I could fix it with a quick song. The urge rose in his chest, quickly followed by thoughts of how he'd failed as a wizard and therefore needed to prove himself once more. The drive almost overwhelmed him, and he almost gave in, but remembering Aino helped him push it down.

The temptation receded like a tide, and when he felt in control again, Jouko took a deep breath. His hands stung, and he looked at them—red and bleeding slightly where he'd gripped the twine while resisting the urge to sing.

He stretched his fingers and moved them about, refusing to entertain the idea that he could end the minor pain with a few notes. The broken bundle would suffice for him tonight, and Papa would get the next one. Jouko would be sure to tie off that one with more care. With sore hands, he'd need to anyway.

After setting the completed vihta on the ground beside him, he turned to work on the next one, slowly and with more care. As he selected cuttings one by one, his mind drifted back to Aino. That was something else he'd forgotten about simple, non-magical chores: they allowed one's mind to wander to places that weren't always welcome.

Yet he didn't let himself push the thoughts away, not when the blame for his sister's absence lay solidly on his shoulders. He deserved every bit of guilt he felt over her predicament.

Was Aino safe? Was she *alive*? He clung to the hope of both.

"Son, where's my vihta?" his mother yelled from the sauna door. She grunted and pulled the door shut with a heavy *thunk* to show her annoyance.

"They're almost ready," Jouko called. With a sigh, he picked up the first two he'd finished—before he'd ruined the third one—and walked over to the sauna.

As soon as he'd turned back to the log, the sauna opened. He glanced over his shoulder in time to see Sanna's arm slip out to grab the two bundles.

Before the door closed, Mama poked her head out. "Finally!" She slammed the door.

Jouko sighed and took his seat on the log once more, where he worked on the last vihta for the night. He glanced up at the sauna, at his mother, whose grating voice rang in his ears.

She hadn't spoken of Vane's death, but she made her feelings on the matter quite clear. She banged pots and pans, broke a few dishes, kicked a chair. She sobbed and wailed over how the family had been so close to fame, so close to power and a prosperous future, only to lose it at the hands of her selfish children. She cried without tears and wailed, rarely stopping for more than a few moments, when no one was about to see her grief.

His search for Aino would take time, and Jouko wanted to leave right away, but his father begged him to stay until morning for the sake of Mama's nerves. The plea was as much for Papa's sake, Jouko was quite certain, so his father wouldn't have to suffer through his mother's rants alone.

Soon the last vihta was complete. He'd made only four tonight. The pile of cuttings still had enough for one more bundle, but Aino wasn't home to need one. He tucked his knife away and picked them up—his broken one and the other for his father.

Aino was right to seek out the Maids. He headed for the washroom side of the sauna, where he'd leave the bundles. If what he'd found in Seppo's study was true, then getting the Maids' help truly had been her only chance. No one, himself included, would have considered Vane's death a possibility.

You are free of him now, Aino, he thought as he set the vihtas beside the sauna.

He intended to go back into the house along the well-worn footpath, but he heard a sound from somewhere near that made him stop and listen. Footsteps? No, not quite. But someone—or something—seemed to be approaching.

Who would come to his family's sauna by the pond without an invitation? No one with the slightest sense of manners would do so, except Vane.

Jouko stiffen. "The singer is dead," he whispered, needing to hear the words. It helped somewhat, but he couldn't rest easy until he knew the source of the sound.

One slow step at a time, he circled the sauna, squinting in the twilight. To his left, some grasses moved; he withdrew his knife and held it out. "Show yourself!"

No answer came, but more movements appeared in the same area, bending grasses. Could it be a squirrel or a bird? The swaying motions indicated a far larger creature.

"I said, show yourself!"

The movement stilled, and a voice hesitantly answered. "I-I have a message."

Jouko clenched the knife handle harder; his pulse quickened. "Who are you?"

"My message is for your family."

"Who are you?"

"I am Kari. My message is about Aino."

"What do you know of my sister?" Jouko cried. He looked all around but could see no source of the voice. "Where are you? Show yourself."

The same noises as before shook the grasses, but they were short and abrupt, not like a man's footsteps at all. The pattern almost seemed like an animal hopping. Sure enough, a hare landed two paces ahead of Jouko and stared at him with intelligent eyes. The animal unnerved him, but Jouko wouldn't be distracted. He continued to look about, but with night falling, he couldn't distinguish between the shapes and shadows about him.

"I am Kari," the hare said.

Jouko started backward and tripped on a stone. He nearly tumbled to the ground in surprise but managed to catch his balance. "You—can speak!"

"I bear a message from your sister for your family," the hare went on, nonplussed.

"How—how—" Jouko couldn't speak, couldn't make sense of what he was witnessing.

He'd heard of talking animals, of course—humans cursed and transformed for one misdeed or another. Jouko had assumed that they were nothing more than cautionary tales intended to encourage children to obey their elders. If Seppo had known about such magic, surely he would have taught his apprentice. But he hadn't, so Jouko never believed them to be real.

A week ago, I didn't believe in immortals, either.

"How?" Kari repeated, his voice even. "While on a sinking ship, I begged the Sun and Moon Sisters to save me. They transformed me into the form you see now."

"I see," Jouko said, though the only words he'd comprehended were *Sun and Moon Sisters*.

"Your sister bade me tell your family what has befallen her."

164

Speaking hare or no, Jouko gathered his wits for Aino's sake. "Tell me."

"Where are your parents?"

"My father is at the house, but my mother and sister are in the sauna."

"Fetch your mother, at least," Kari said.

Jouko hurried to the front of the sauna and knocked loudly. "Mama! We have a messenger with news of Aino. Come quickly!"

The door flew open, and his mother emerged around the corner of the sauna, tying a sash about her robe as she hurried toward the path. "Aino? Where is she?" Mama looked about, but her step came up short when she saw no one outside. Confusion blanketed her face.

Sanna appeared behind her, tugging her shift on, and spoke the question they both had. "You said there was a messenger."

Jouko nodded at the hare. "Tell us."

"You are Aino's mother?" Kari asked.

"It speaks!" Mama made a strangled noise and jumped back. Jouko had to catch her so she wouldn't fall.

"Yes, I speak," Kari said evenly. "Your daughter sought out the Sun and Moon Sisters to save herself from Vane."

"Did she find them? Do they know where she lives?" Mama clutched her robe with one hand, looking pale and ready to collapse from fright.

"She found them," the hare said. "The Maids agreed to keep her from Vane's hands."

"What if they come for me?" Mama fanned her face with one hand.

"Their way of saving her from Vane," Kari went on, "was to turn her into a fish."

This time Jouko spoke out. "A fish?" he said in as much shock as dismay.

"She swims in the ocean," Kari said. "You should also know that the singer is yet alive."

"No," Jouko said, shaking his head again and again, as if that would change reality. "I killed him. He dropped into the sea and drowned—" It was the only time he'd sung since the duel, and he'd done so to free his sister, just as he'd vowed. Yet he'd failed again? "How do you know?" He had to struggle to keep his voice from cracking with tears.

"I know because the trees have whispered it to me. His claim on her in human form still holds, but so long as she remains a fish, he cannot take her."

Jouko's mind spun in circles. He tried to think rationally as Seppo had taught him, to not allow his emotions to interfere with reason. But the old lessons were far harder to apply when the life of your sister hung in the balance.

His mother turned to Jouko and sagged into his arms. "What have I done?" A sob crept up her throat and escaped in a keening cry. "The Maids may come destroy me, and now Vane won't want Aino. Oh, my sweet Aino! What have I done?"

Jouko led her to a stump, where she collapsed, hands covering her face as she sobbed. She rocked back and forth. "Aino, my baby." Tears the size of plump peas tumbled down her cheeks and wet her robe. "I should never have told her who she must marry. It is not a mother's right. If only someone could save her." She lifted her face abruptly and gripped Jouko's wrists. "You must do it. If anyone in the world can do such a thing, it is you—you have the magic, the skill, to bring her home to me."

His throat tightened at her plea. Twice he'd failed against Vane. Would a third attempt mean death for Aino?

It will mean death for me, but that matters not if Aino is free.

He gently removed his mother's hands and cupped her face between his own. "I will find Aino, and I will bring her home." He made the promise without any idea of how—or if he would keep it.

166

Chapter Eighteen

Jouko faced Kari. "Can you lead me to Aino? I must find her."

The hare made one big hop and turned back. "Come," he said.

Without thought, without food, or water, or supplies of any kind beyond the knife at his belt, Jouko ran after the hare, following him by the light of the moon. Into the woods they went, quickly leaving paths and going through the thick brush and trees. He ran as fast as he could, determined to keep up with Kari, to follow the one who could lead him to his sister.

Soon they passed the Sorsa family's homestead, and he instinctively called after Kari. "Stop!"

The hare bounded forward several times and then stopped. "We must hurry."

"Aino's intended needs to hear what has happened—and not from my mother."

After a brief moment of consideration, Kari nodded. "Be quick. I must return to the Sisters before they notice my absence."

"I'll hurry," Jouko said. "It's through those trees."

"I'll wait here," Kari said. "But not for long. I might have already been away too long."

"I won't be but a moment," Jouko assured him.

He sprinted the whole way to Paavo's bedroom window, then rapped against the closed shutter. "Paavo!" He looked back to be sure Kari hadn't left, but couldn't make out his shape in the darkness of the forest. He rapped again. "I have word of Aino!"

The shutter opened, and Paavo appeared at the window. "What is it? Tell me!"

"Come outside, and I'll explain. Wear boots."

ANNETTE LYON

Within moments, a wide-eyed Paavo had come out and heard the news. As expected, he wanted to come along. Soon the two young men ran, Jouko leading the way. He expected Kari to speak, but instead, the hare bounded off. The boys ran and ran on, often losing sight of the hare. More than once, Jouko was on the verge of giving up hope and calling for Kari, only for the hare to materialize ahead, paw raised to his mouth as if to insist they remain silent.

Kari appeared antsy to reach his destination and could have gone faster, Jouko was sure. At times, he slowed down to give the men time to find him or catch up, but the pace was more than the two men could bear for much longer.

"I can't—go—on—" Paavo gasped.

"Neither—can—I."

No matter that they were both strong young men; within a few moments, they would both collapse to the forest floor.

I must sing, Jouko realized with dismay. A song of endurance and physical strength to keep him and Paavo moving. Kari certainly wouldn't stop.

I don't want to sing, but I must to help Aino.

He'd kept his vow after the duel to not sing unless it helped Aino. Last time he'd sung, he'd ambushed Vane and believed he'd succeeded. Instead, he'd failed Aino again.

Let this song help me find her. I cannot fail her a third time.

Jouko tapped his companion on the arm and gestured for them to slow down. Paavo gratefully stopped and leaned over, hands on his legs, gasping. After catching his own breath, Jouko closed his eyes and inhaled from deep inside. The tones came out weak, the words breathy, but though imperfect, the spell was enough to give them both a boost in stamina.

Somehow Jouko kept singing, and Kari remained in view for the rest of their journey. The sky began lightening black to dark blue, then gray to pale yellow with the dawn. Jouko could scarcely keep his eyes open and legs moving, and the song stumbled, along with his feet. He couldn't sing another note. If he'd had the strength, it wouldn't have mattered; he'd sung so long that his throat was raw.

"I can't—"

"You don't have to." Paavo reached under Jouko's arms and supported his weight. "I can help you now. We must go on."

In spite of his exhaustion and inability to sing, Jouko tried to hum, hoping that the song of presence would help even the slightest bit in keeping their minds awake and their bodies alert.

As the sun crested the horizon, Jouko's toe caught a rock. He fell from Paavo's grasp, and as he reached out to catch himself, he scraped his palm on a dead juniper log. He couldn't get up. He lay there, unable to speak, sing, or even hum.

If they lost Kari now, their efforts to find Aino would be for naught. Jouko lacked the strength to ask Kari to wait.

Paavo dropped to the ground too. "I can't go on," he said in defeat.

Somehow Jouko pushed himself to his knees but had to support himself on the log. He looked about for sign of Kari but saw none. "Do you see him?"

Following his example, Paavo worked his way to his knees. They both craned their necks this way and that. "I don't see him."

They were lost. They hadn't found Aino, and they might starve to death without a crumb to eat or a drop to drink. Jouko's heart dropped to his boots. He shouldn't have sung; it hadn't helped Aino at all. Better to have remained silent than sing and run all night, only to have his parents lose a second child.

Wordlessly, Paavo pointed. "There," he said, but without confidence.

Jouko followed the direction he pointed. Some distance away, hardly distinguishable from the trees, was the hare, standing still. He looked back at them and brought a paw to his mouth as if to signal silence, then pointed toward a stone outcropping that stretched from the shore to water beyond—a lake or the sea, he didn't know.

They quietly moved forward, step by careful step. A lone boat floated on the water not too far from shore. An old man with a bushy beard sat inside, singing. His voice was low and gravelly—and one Jouko would never forget.

Vane.

Chills went through him. His jaw clenched as he stood there, wanting to jump into the water to kill the old man despite his fatigue. Reason prevailed; he didn't take a step, didn't speak a word or sing a note.

Vane's rod dangled in the water, presumably to catch breakfast. But he didn't sing to draw in a catch. Rather, he sang for a way to find his lost love. His Aino.

She is not your love. Jouko seethed at the assertion.

"Listen," Kari whispered.

"To what?" Jouko said through his teeth. "To the old man claiming he cares one whit about my sister?"

"His song could lead you to her," Kari said.

"His—" Jouko's middle leapt with hope. He looked at the hare and grinned. The song hadn't seemed like a charm, only an old man's tortured wishes.

But what if the song was magical? If any power would draw Aino to a wizard, it would be one that Vane possessed. Only a day ago, Jouko would have pled for such a song to not exist. Now he prayed it did, and that it would indeed draw Aino to the old man.

He and Paavo each gripped a tree limb and watched.

Chapter Nineteen

Slowly, the fish swam mindlessly through the salty sea-water. Usually she swam alone, but sometimes with a small school of other fish, but somehow knew she didn't belong with them. Through her clouded mind, she noticed that any time she met another fish or a sea maid, they glanced below her mouth. They often swam away, as if what they'd seen there made them uneasy.

What they could see there, she didn't know. Sometimes a glimpse of memory swished by, like thin lace that flew past her vision and vanished. She should remember what they saw, but didn't.

At times her strength dipped so low that her belly grazed tops of the seaweed. Other times she skimmed the surface, where the sun broke through and warmed the water.

She often went to an outcropping that held a writ rock, never knowing why she felt drawn to that spot. As with the curious reactions of others to whatever they saw below her mouth, she had a sense that she should remember the significance of the writ rock, if nothing else than to remember why she knew it was called that.

Sometimes she had a dream-like image of the writ rock sinking, of panic and wetness and being thrown through the air and into the water. Such a daydream made no sense; why would a fish fear the water? How would a fish know anything other than wetness?

She swam in wide circles and curlicue patterns, enjoying currents that took her one direction before she broke away and drifted with another. The water had gotten warmer with the lengthening days. The water refreshed her as it slid past her scales.

Once more, she found herself near the shoreline, close to the writ rock. She'd gone there often without intending to, and here she'd come again. As she had many times, she peered up through the water and pondered. Why did the outcropping itself evoke such powerful emotions in her? Why did she have images of the writ rock and fear of the water?

Such questions made her sad, so she flipped about and swam away. Then she swam as fast as she could and jumped through the surface, into the air, before plunging into the salty sea again.

She found jumping to be most enjoyable and intended to do it again. But before she could, something caught her attention. It dangled in the water—light brown, like the soil at the bottom of the sea, only lighter. The ends were pointed, like the tops of some plants. Curious, she swam around the object.

What is it? She swam around it again.

What might it taste like? Another circuit, and she decided to taste the unusual object. But as she opened her mouth, an idea struck her hard, like a wave.

Don't. It could kill you.

She closed her mouth and looked around, feeling strange. Where had the words come from? No matter, as they made no sense. What kind of word was *kill?* She hadn't eaten for hours, and here she had what was likely a brown bug before her, waiting to be eaten. She might experience a different taste that would be exciting, fun.

Her attention was interrupted again, this time by a sound coming through the water above her. It was distorted and unclear, mesmerizing. She looked at the pointy object and wanted to taste it even more. She drew closer to it, closer, and closer still, until she opened her mouth around it and tried to swallow.

A sudden jerk sent a shock of pain through her throat. Pain. Searing pain. She suddenly remembered another fish doing this same thing, then being drawn out of the sea. Never returning.

Killed. She knew what that meant now.

That's a lure. The term of the pointy object returned with force, as did the purpose of it.

Other memories came back too, hazy at first, but quickly resolving into clear pictures.

I'm not a fish! She knew that truth as well as anything, but the knowledge didn't stop her from being drawn up, out of the water, by the fishing line. The lure still pierced the back of her throat and tore the flesh.

On the surface, she gasped for breath as death pressed on her small body. Water. She needed water. Her body flopped about in someone's heavily calloused, aging hands.

Aino. That is my name. The memory flooded back as another, horrifying realization washed over her.

He'll kill me, just as I killed hundreds of fish as a woman. I'm human!

She flailed harder in the man's hands, fighting to return to the water now, or she would die. As she fought, her body twisted and turned. One eye landed on her captor—and felt instantly paralyzed.

Vane.

Pulse thudding in her head, Aino desperately fought to get away, but the wizard's grasp held fast.

"Quite a fighter you are," the old man said. "You won't get away so . . ." His voice trailed off. He lowered his head, brow furrowed. "What is this?" He touched the spot below her mouth that others stared at. And while she wanted to kick and spit at him as a human could, and to never feel his touch again, the moment gave her another memory.

My solki! She remembered Paavo—his face, his voice, his kisses. Her love for him. Aino fought harder yet, refusing to surrender now that she knew who she was and what had brought her here. *Better to be a fish than Vane's captive wife.*

"The gods have answered my song," Vane said in awe. "I've found my Aino at last."

I am not yours. I will never be yours. She twisted about, released the lure, and with a final jerk, escaped Vane's hands.

Flying in an arc toward the sea, she looked over her shoulder—for, because of his song to the gods, in that split moment, she *had* a shoulder again. She had her golden-red hair that brushed against her back. She had legs and arms and swam away, kicking her legs.

Vane reached over the edge of his boat. His hand grazed her foot as she slipped out of his reach. "Aino, my love!" he cried, but once again she'd become a fish. Her gills opened and closed frantically, breathing as fast as she could. But above her, Vane still called for her. "I sang you to me. Don't leave!"

Once again, Aino was free from Vane.

Once again, she was a fish.

Chapter Twenty

"Aino, come back!" Vane's cry felt like sharp talons scratching her back. "You belong to me. We shall be wed and live together in happiness."

Keeping her distance, Aino turned about with her tail and fins and yelled. "I will *never* wed you!"

She cared nothing for other possible futures that awaited her. Let her forget who she was. That would likely happen again quickly. Let another fisherman catch and kill her. Far better to die a mindless fish than to be trapped as a woman for decades, forced to be the wife of Old Reliable Vane.

"You would prefer to swim with the fish?" Vane asked, incredulous. "How can you think that a life in the cold and salty sea would be better than the one I can give you?"

"Because it means choosing my own fate. And I choose the sea." Her tail swished side to side. She would probably succumb to temptation with the next lure she came across. If she had to die a fish, better for it to happen without a knowledge of who she'd been or how she'd loved Paavo and wanted to be *his* wife.

"But I have riches and wealth." Vane gesticulated wildly, as if he expected her to change her mind, to jump into his arms after all. "You will always have money. A house larger than your greatest fantasies. You will be warm and fed all year long, even in the coldest and darkest of winters. You will have grand clothing and jewelry. You will be the envy of all women."

"I do not want money or jewelry or others' envy. I want the life *I* choose." She did not care if Vane understood or heard her from the water, only that she was free of him. The Sisters did give her that.

For now, she still wanted Paavo. She ached for him. Wanted to feel his arms around her, and wrap her human arms around him one last time.

"I can turn you back into a girl," Vane insisted. "You know that I am powerful. I can transform the spell of immortals just as they transformed mine."

Aino swam in a tight circle. She tried to think but found it dreadfully hard.

"That's right," Vane said. "I know how you became a fish. And you know I have more magic than any other wizard, including your dear brother, who tried to kill me."

His words sent a flurry of emotions through Aino, but she couldn't comprehend them all, so she kept swimming around and around. Jouko tried to kill Vane? How? Was her brother dead?

"Alas," Vane went on, "you asked for the spell that made you a fish, didn't you? Yes, you did, because the Sun and Moon Maids never interfere with mortals unless someone begs them to. Because you asked for their help, I cannot transform their magic without your consent, just as they couldn't have transformed mine if you hadn't requested it."

"Go away," Aino said, hating how muddled her mind was getting. "Go. Now."

"Would you like me to make you human again?" Vane asked. "Say yes—that one word—and you will again have arms and legs and pretty red hair. You will be able to run and dance and eat strawberries."

His deep voice made Aino swim more slowly; her circles became less frantic. She felt almost sleepy, and as he spoke, she remembered what being a woman was like. Remembered the taste of wild berries. Dancing at the Midsummer Night festival. Kissing Paavo.

"One simple word." Vane no longer sounded desperate, but kind and understanding. "Say yes, and I will make you human again. You will be able to have all of the pleasures you've ever dreamed of." His voice softened even more. "Say yes, Aino. Say *yes*."

Her tail and fins went still. She imagined warm summer days, crackling fires in winter, knitting warm socks, freshly baked bread. She poked her head above the surface, studying

Vane's face. He didn't look terrible anymore. He almost looked fatherly.

"You'll sing me human?"

"Just say yes."

"And then what?"

"You can dance and eat berries, and—"

"And will I be free?" Her human memories kept tickling the back of her mind.

"Free from the sea, yes. Free from those hard scales and cold saltwater."

"Free from *you*?"

Vane's face tightened, and he sat back in his boat. "I will sing you human," he repeated.

"No," Aino said. "If I agreed, you would claim me as your bride, and I will not be forced to be your companion." She swished her head side to side. "No. No!"

Vane gestured toward the ocean. "You would rather live like this?" His brows knit together, creating a deep furrow between them. His top lip curled with fury.

What could he do with that fury when his wife didn't bend to his every wish? She would never bow to his wishes. Not now when she had the simple power to withhold herself from him. In a way, that made her, a little fish, stronger than the greatest wizard ever known.

"Renounce your claim on me," Aino said. Her tail flipped side to side, turning the sea frothy.

"Never," Vane growled.

"It does not matter. I will never be yours either way." She meant the words, but they still caused her pain. She would remain a fish, but at least she would be *free*. She would leave this part of the ocean and swim far away, never to see her family again, never to kiss Paavo or hear his voice. Never to enjoy the pleasures of feeling rain on her face, tasting the burst of fresh blueberries, hearing birds in the trees.

"Come, come," the wizard said, as if cajoling a child.

"Free me from your claim, or I will swim away and remain a fish for all of my remaining days, however few they may be." She hovered just out of Vane's reach. Would he refuse to release her out of spite? When he realized he had no hope of wedding her, would he give in?

177

He settled back in his boat and rowed for the rocky shore. Aino followed warily, staying out of reach but wanting to be sure he left.

The boat creaked as it made landfall. Vane climbed out and pulled the craft from the water. But he didn't depart. He sat on the writ rock, hands on his thighs, and gazed toward the sea, clearly unaware that Aino the fish had followed and watched him from behind some kelp.

After some time, his head lowered as if he contemplated a complicated puzzle. Did he have a kind spot in his heart, or would his revenge keep her bound?

A figure appeared behind Vane, hopping about on the stony outcropping. Kari had returned. Aino's tail swished faster. She prayed he wouldn't speak to her and betray her presence.

"You look rather dejected," the hare said to Vane. He hopped over to the old man and gazed out over the sea as well.

The old man glanced at Kari—apparently not at all surprised at his ability to speak—and shrugged. "You would be right."

"Lady trouble?" The hare didn't look at Vane, and his voice betrayed nothing of his knowledge of Aino or how she was connected to the man at his side.

Clever hare.

"What other kind of trouble is there?" Vane chuckled, but sadness in his face belied the sunny tone. The man looked sincerely distraught. Perhaps he was lonely and genuinely wanted a companion. His way of getting one left something to be desired, but she pitied his dreary, solitary life, if that's what he had.

"Perhaps if you had another lady to think on," Kari suggested, "the one on your mind would not bother you so."

He drew a hand down his leathery, tired face. "If a simple farm girl won't have me, who will?"

"There are rumors . . ." Kari's voiced trailed off, and he threw a sideways look at Vane, who took the bait.

"What kind of rumors?"

"Oh, I've heard the trees whispering that the Louhi is seeking a groom for her eldest daughter."

178

"What has that to do with me?" Vane's brooding eyes stared out at the horizon.

Kari's ears shifted, and he moved a bit closer to the wizard. "The winds say that many men have vied for her hand—many have *sung* for her hand and performed feats to prove their worth—but she will have none of them. And while her mother Louhi despises you"—Vane grunted in annoyance but agreement—"her daughter says that every suitor falls short . . . of the legendary Vane."

"She has said this?" He sat a bit straighter. "The eldest maid of the north, daughter of Louhi, has said she wants . . . *me?*"

"She has."

Vane's gaze returned to the water, his eyes bright. Aino swam in eager circles, trying to keep her hopes from being raised too high—and trying not to splash, so he wouldn't note her presence.

"If half the stories are true of her boundless beauty, you would be a fool not to seek her out," Kari went on, waving a paw casually. "Locks like silken honey, skin like cream, voice like summer rain."

The old man began nodding. Aino felt her insides lurch with fear, hope, and the desperate need to know what her future held.

"I need a companion to spend my days with," Vane said. "If one of the Maids of the North is willing, and if Louhi doesn't object . . ."

"She is eager to see her daughter wed," Kari interjected. "Besides, you've vied for her daughter's hand before, have you not? Louhi knows what mettle you are made of."

"True enough." The singer tapped his lips with one finger as he contemplated. He raised an eyebrow. "If I sing to the trees, and they deny the rumors, I will curse you to a fate worse than death itself."

"Naturally," Kari said with an airy tone. "Ask the trees, the immortals, anyone you wish. Louhi *is* looking for a man to wed her eldest daughter. Thus far, all have fallen short of your performance last time she sought a groom for her child. Granted, to vie for her hand, you'd have to rid yourself of any other bonds to a woman, but it sounds as if you'd happily do so to rid yourself of you 'lady trouble.'"

The words made so much sense that Aino couldn't tell whether the hare was bluffing.

After a long moment that felt tortuous to Aino, the old man stood and raised his hands to his mouth. "Aino!" he called. "Come!"

A flutter erupted in her chest. She could hardly swim straight. *Please, don't let this be a trick,* she prayed to the gods. *Don't let him catch me.*

She didn't come right up to the edge of the water; that would be too dangerous. But she made sure the wizard could see her. "I am here, Vane. What do you want?"

The singer filled his lungs.

Sing I now, Vane of story,
powerful Vane.

His deep voice vibrated through the water. For a moment, Aino worried about what he would say next—might he change his mind and curse her?

Aino is not mine.
My claim is hereby gone.
No more do spells hold her to me.
Her singer brother's likewise free.
Nevermore will I seek her hand.
Nevermore.

Vane held the last note until he ran out of breath and his head drooped.

For Aino, the weight of worry lifted. She could feel the spell loosening its grasp and setting her free. She remained a fish. But she was free. She no longer feared the wizard.

She pushed her head through the salty surface. "I hope you find joy and happiness," she said to Vane, and surprised herself by meaning the words.

The old man looked down at her. He smiled and rubbed the back of his hand across one eye—had he been crying?

"Goodbye, Aino. May you have a good life in the sea." He headed for the forest.

"Kari, you lied to save me," Aino said. "How did you summon the courage? He could still curse you."

"Technically, I did not lie," Kari said with a smile. "Louhi *is* searching for a man to marry her eldest. The trees will confirm that when he asks, as I have no doubt he will. But Louhi will never give her consent."

Aino couldn't help but laugh, though it came out as a squeak and a flutter of her fins. "In that case, you did something no one thought possible: you outwitted Old Reliable," she said. "I am in your debt. Thank you."

"You are most welcome," he said. "I did only what I hope someone would do for me if given the chance. I, too, wish to be free one day." He gave her a sad smile.

Before Vane crossed the tree line and disappeared from view, he paused and looked back. She and Kari lapsed into silence as they watched.

"Aino, I cannot turn you human again. If I were to do so now, I would be too tempted to steal, to find a way to make you my wife." He hooked his thumbs on his belt and furrowed his brow, looking perturbed. "I am not a good man. Leaving you a fish may be the noblest act I ever do. Farewell. May you find happiness, be it among the reeds."

Chapter Twenty-One

Jouko could scarcely believe what he'd just witnessed from the cover of the trees.

At his side, Paavo leaned close. "That was *Vane*." They both knew who the man was, of course, but the fact made seeing him no less amazing. They watched him trudge away, soon enveloped by the forest.

Vane had left, with no intention of coming back.

The two young men held still for several minutes in an unspoken agreement. Neither said a word until they were sure Vane was really gone.

The first to speak was Paavo. "Do you think he's really heading north?"

"I hope so," Jouko said. "But he'll be rejected again. Then what?"

Paavo's head came around sharply. "You think Kari was bluffing?" Fear tinged his voice.

All Jouko could do was shrug. "Can you imagine Louhi's daughter agreeing to marrying him?"

Paavo's shoulders rose and then fell. "Not all women are as determined as your sister to forge their own paths."

"True. Aino is many things, but easily swayed is not one of them." Jouko smiled and clapped Paavo on the back. "Come."

Jouko led the way along a faint path, with Paavo close behind. When he stepped onto the elongated rock, there was the hare with his back to the shore. "We saw Vane leave," he said. "What happened? Is my sister truly free?"

Kari turned and looked at Jouko in acknowledgment but then turned away. "Vane revoked his claim, yes."

After a night of running, both men nearly collapsed with relief at the confirmation.

"Where is she?" Jouko asked at the same time Paavo said, "My sweet Aino is free?"

"Free," Kari said. "But, as you see, still a fish." He gestured to the water, where a pretty fish swam in figure eights, seemingly unaware of the men on the shore.

"Thank you," Paavo said. He dropped to his knees before Kari. "However you did it!"

The hare scratched behind one ear with a paw. "To be honest, in part, I helped for a selfish reason."

Jouko came closer, his guard up again. Magic seemed to always come with a price, one, he learned, not always worth paying. "What kind of selfish reason?"

"I've told you how the forest speaks to me."

"Yes," Jouko said cautiously.

"The cuckoos say you are a great singer. That you bested Vane."

"That is a lie." Jouko said. Never again would he boast or bend truths to polish his ego. "Our first meeting, I lost a duel. On our second, I tried to kill him and thought I did. But as you know, he lives."

"Yes, he lives," the hare repeated. He turned from the sea and gazed into Jouko's eyes. "But still, you bested him."

"I don't understand," Jouko said. "How did I—"

"Where is Aino?" Paavo interrupted.

Though Jouko knew where she was, he let the hare explain. Aino was the reason for his journey, the entire purpose of everything he'd done for the last several days. And while Vane had left, she remained charmed, unable to live a full life.

Instead of explaining, the hare merely pointed at the rippling ocean again. "See for yourself."

Paavo leaned over and peered into the water, but he didn't seem to grasp what the others already knew, that Aino was literally a fish.

"I'm here," came a voice. Aino's, yet not hers. The voice was high and thin, but recognizable all the same. A fish swam closer, stirring up water and silt around it. The design below the mouth was unmistakable—a circle with a lingonberry design around it.

"Her solki," Paavo breathed.

183

Jouko's eyes burned at the sight. "It *is* you." He'd had no doubt, but seeing her made everything both harder to believe and more real at the same time.

"I'm free!" Her voice seemed to ripple through the water. "Vane renounced his claim. I'm free to marry. Now that the contract is void, you can sing me back to my human form, can't you?"

"I—" Jouko's throat constricted with mixed joy and anxiety. He'd transformed plenty of objects over the years—a hammer into a spade, a ball of yarn into mittens. Even a rat into a dog. But a fish into a human? Into his *sister*? Transforming the spell of an immortal?

"Perhaps," he said. "But I should go to Seppo's to study more, or I fear I won't do it right, and—"

"Try me first," Kari interjected. The men turned to the hare in surprise. "I, too, have been transformed. If you can transform me back into a man, I will be indebted to you for the rest of my life. 'Tis the selfish reason I referred to. The Maids refuse to change me back, but you could. At least try."

"What if I fail?"

"Then I remain a hare."

"Or you die," Jouko said. "I cannot have the death of a soothsayer on my shoulders."

Kari smiled. "It would but be the death of a hare. And if you succeed, you will have returned me to life." He hopped closer to Jouko. "Try. That is all I ask."

"Yes, try," Aino said. She swam around some reeds and back again.

they did save you

Despite the morning chill, sweat formed on Jouko's neck and forehead. "What if I turn you into something else, like a rat or a spider? What if I kill Kari?"

He didn't voice his greater fear: *What if I manage to transform Kari but kill my sister?*

Paavo grabbed Jouko by the shoulders. "You can do this. You can and you must. Do it for your sister."

"But I'm not—"

"Yes, you *are* good enough. The fact that you've learned humility shows that you're open to learning and don't know everything about magic. You are Kari's and Aino's best hope."

Jouko tried to believe his friend's words, but doubts seemed to build faster storm clouds, darkening his mind. He sat on the rock and watched the fish that was Aino swim about.

Somehow without a sound, Kari went to Jouko's side. "You must at least try to save your sister," Kari said. "You owe her that much." He paused as if about to say what Jouko already knew: that Aino's becoming a fish was his fault. To Kari's credit, he said no such thing. Instead he added, "You are one of the few singers who have studied under the great Seppo Ilmarinen, forger of the sampo. If anyone can bring Aino back, you can. Do it for the love you have for her."

His breath staggered and uneven, Jouko closed his eyes. A tear ran down one cheek. Paavo and Kari were right; he had to try for Aino's sake. Aside from the old wizard and Seppo Ilmarinen himself, Jouko was one of the few people living who had the skill to *perhaps* change Aino back into the young woman she'd been before.

Jouko finally nodded. "I'll try." He nodded again, then again, as if doing so would increase his courage. Palms wet with perspiration, his mind whirled with the complexities required for this type of transformation. He didn't know much about how fish bodies were made, let alone a woman's. But first, he'd attempt hare to human.

Creating a nail from a piece of discarded metal was far simpler than turning an animal into a human with a soul. Jouko brought his palms together and the edge of his hands against his face to help him concentrate. He imagined himself back in the library, memorizing words and melodies and creating his own.

With a deep breath, he lowered his hands, turned to Kari, and opened his mouth. The raw throat of before was gone. His notes were clear and perfect, the tone warm. Yet the hare cried out in pain. Jouko's eyes widened, and a note cracked.

Kari fell to the rock and moaned. But he was also changing; his legs and arms lengthened, and his fur smoothed into skin. Encouraged, Jouko quickly recovered and continued singing. Paws turned into hands and fingers. The long ears pulled into the top of his head, as did the whiskers. Within moments, a man of fifty years lay on the stone, panting heavily. He wore a ragged shirt and a pair of equally trousers.

"I'm—I'm a man!" The words came out as a strangled sob as Kari the man pushed up from the ground. He stared at his hands, moved his fingers, touched his face, then scrambled to his feet. "I never imagined I'd be so happy to see my old clothes again. Thank you! I thank you with every part of my being." He threw his arms around Jouko and hugged him hard.

Jouko embraced him back, feeling the wave of emotion from Kari as his own body trembled from the sheer amount of power he'd used.

"I'm a *man*." Kari released Jouko. Tears streamed down his cheeks. "You can bring back your sister, too."

Jouko looked at the fish again. His knees felt ready to knock into each other. A hare to a human was simpler than a fish to a human. Besides, he was already fatigued. What if, in his weakness, he made a mistake?

"You did it once already," Paavo said. "You can do it a second time."

But this time mattered more to Jouko, and it would be so much more complicated. One wrong note could kill his sister. He would be to blame for Aino's demise. And he'd never forgive himself.

I am already to blame, he thought. *I must try, or I'll live with the shame all my days.*

"You *will* bring her back," Paavo said.

After a deep breath, Jouko closed his eyes again to eliminate distractions. As before, he imagined himself in the library, with his master Seppo at his side, guiding his creation of a new song. He pictured Aino—her golden-red hair, fair skin, blue eyes. When he felt as ready as he could expect to, he sang.

Cries of agony broke the stillness. This time Jouko kept his voice strong. He refused to think about the pain Aino had to be experiencing as her body changed and stretched and grew. He kept his lids closed, for his song might falter if he witnessed her suffering.

After the first verse, he took another deep breath and continued with the next stage, and made it stronger, more decisive. He recalled a complex chant Seppo had taught him only once. Somehow, he remembered it by heart and sang it boldly to quicken both Aino's body and mind.

When he finished the song, Jouko could hardly breathe or stand. He leaned over, panting, holding himself up by leaning on the writ rock. He was nearly bowled over by someone throwing their arms about his neck.

Aino.

His eyes flew open, and he held her close. She was completely dry, as was her hair. When he released her, and looked her over, she looked happy, never more radiant, though she wore only her plain old shift.

"I will never again be so selfish," Jouko said, holding her hands. "My pride is nothing without your happiness."

Paavo stepped forward and touched her arm. At that, she released her brother and embraced her beloved.

"Hold me," she said, pressing her face into his neck.

They embraced tightly, each weeping for joy and relief. He kissed her cheek. She lifted her face and leaned close to kiss his lips. She sighed as if savoring the sensations of being human. Paavo slowly pulled back and touched the solki, once again on its blue ribbon around her neck.

Her hand joined his on the solki, sign of their love and betrothal. "I would give much to be your wife today."

Kari cleared his throat, making Aino and Paavo look over. "You know, as a tietäjä, I am a soothsayer, a seer, a sage, and . . ." He shot a grin at them. "A priest. Performing a marriage would be a start in repaying you for the gift of my life."

"Yes. Please do," Jouko said eagerly. But then he turned to his sister, realizing his rash mistake. "That is, Aino, if marrying Paavo here today is what *you* wish."

"It is," she said, then planted a kiss on his cheek. "And you are wise to have asked."

"I am hardheaded, but I can learn." He pressed a kiss to her forehead.

Aino and Paavo stood side by side, hands clasped together, arms held out before Kari. He spoke the simple ceremony. Jouko stood as the sole witness. Aino stole a glance at him, and he grinned, happier than he could remember being. He could have sung all the day long in celebration, praising the gods.

"Now go and begin a new life together," Kari said.

"What will you do?" Aino asked him. "Where will you go?"

"I go home. And I pray that my wife yet lives." He stepped forward and looked from across the group of three. "If I can ever be of service to you again, call for me."

Aino lifted a hand and asked, "How will we find you?"

The priest walked toward the trees and called over his shoulder. "Talk to the trees. They'll know."

Leaning into Paavo's embrace and fingering the solki, Aino wondered aloud, "What do you think my mother will say when she discovers that I am now the wife of a fur merchant?"

"First, she'll pace the kitchen," Jouko said. "She'll have to decide whether to die of horror or dance for joy."

Aino laughed in agreement. She didn't particularly care what her mother's response would be.

"But first," Jouko said more seriously, "Mama will embrace you with relief and joy because you are alive and well." He placed a hand on Paavo's shoulder. "Most importantly, I believe she will be glad to know that her daughter is happy because she chose her husband and loves him."

Aino took her husband's hand on one side and her brother's hand on the other. She squeezed both. "And I *am* happy," she said, "Happier than I could have ever dreamed."

Acknowledgments

I am one of the lucky people born of Finnish ancestry. In my case, it's through my mother, who was born and raised in Helsinki. I am equally lucky to have lived in Finland for three years in my youth. During that time, I attended public school and learned the language.

My father has long had a love for Finland, its language, and its literature, and that love not only led to my parents' marriage but also to my exposure to *Kalevala* stories at a young age. Without that rich upbringing, this book would never have been written.

I'd never considered writing something directly inspired by Finnish mythology until, on a flight to Finland in 2008, I read *New York Times* bestselling author Jessica Day George's *Sun and Moon, Ice and Snow*, a retelling of a Norwegian myth. By the time the plane landed, I was on fire with the idea of writing a story about Finland. That feeling lasted the entire trip and colored each day of it.

Even so, the book took years to draft and complete. It underwent many revisions, and often got pushed to the back burner because of other obligations and deadlines.

As a result, I owe an enormous debt to the Mastermind Dream Team at Tribalry for giving me the shove I needed to get *Song Breaker* into the world at last. Thanks to Sarah, Wendy, Shar, Marko, Dave, and Joanna!

I am deeply grateful to dear writing friends and colleagues who read different drafts, gave encouragement, and always kept me going: Luisa Perkins, Robison Wells, Sarah M. Eden, Michele Paige Holmes, Heather B. Moore, Jeff Savage, and the late Lu Ann Brobst Staheli.

Thanks to critique partner Julie Bellon read not one but *two* versions and gave me so many helpful notes and suggestions.

And finally, thank you to Mel Henderson, Samantha Lyon, Mel Luthy, and Anne Luthy for notating and proofing.

I couldn't have done it without you all!

About the Author

Annette Lyon is a *USA Today* bestselling author, a 5-time Best of State medalist for novels and short stories in Utah, and a Whitney Award winner. She's had success as a professional editor and in newspaper, magazine, and technical writing, but her first love has always been writing fiction. She's a cum laude graduate from BYU with a degree in English and has authored over a dozen books, including the Whitney Award-winning *Band of Sisters*, a chocolate cookbook, and a grammar guide. She is a regular contributor to and the former editor of the *Timeless Romance Anthology* series. She has received five publication awards from the League of Utah Writers, including the Silver Quill, and she's one of the four coauthors of the *Newport Ladies Book Club* series. Annette is represented by Heather Karpas at ICM Partners.

Find her online:
WEBSITE: AnnetteLyon.com
FACEBOOK: Facebook.com/AnnetteLyon
TWITTER: Twitter.com/AnnetteLyon
INSTAGRAM: Instagram.com/Annette.Lyon
BLOG: blog.annettelyon.com

51884988R00115

Made in the USA
San Bernardino, CA
04 August 2017